FALLIN'
FOR A
Jamaican
KING
2

A NOVEL BY

CANDY MOORE

Royalty Publishing House is now accepting manuscripts from aspiring or experienced urban romance authors!

WHAT MAY PLACE YOU ABOVE THE REST:

Heroes who are the ultimate book bae: strong-willed, maybe a little rough around the edges but willing to risk it all for the woman he loves.

Heroines who are the ultimate match: the girl next door type, not perfect - has her faults but is still a decent person. One who is willing to risk it all for the man she loves.

The rest is up to you! Just be creative, think out of the box, keep it sexy and intriguing!

If you'd like to join the Royal family, send us the first 15K words (60 pages) of your completed manuscript to submissions@royaltypublishing-house.com

Synopsis

Samantha thought she was finally going to get the type of life she dreamed of. She was going to have the devoted husband and she was about to start her family. Well, at least that's what Adam told her, only thing was…he lied!

Samantha is back to square one with her cheating husband; only this time, she doesn't have her King.

King has reverted to his old ways again after Samantha broke his heart. He has given his heart to the streets again, until he learns someone is trying to take his spot as King of the streets.

In this finale, King and Adam are about to vie not only for the streets, but they are about to compete for Samantha's heart!

Samantha

I sat and nibbled on my dry toast with absolutely no interest. I looked around the kitchen as I flipped through the newspapers. I heard the footsteps of my husband approaching and I reached for my cup of coffee and took a sip just as he entered our kitchen.

"What? You didn't make me any breakfast?" he asked, as he walked to where I sat and looked down at me as if I had a lot of nerve not to prepare him something.

"Do I look like I made you any breakfast?" I replied, as I glared at him, holding the dry toast to my lips preparing to bite into the dry dough.

"The least you could have done was made me a cup of coffee, with your selfish ass." *The nerve of this no-good motherfucker*, I thought angrily to myself as we stared each other down.

"Make your own damn coffee Adam," I said, with as much malice in my voice that I could express to him. His facial features changed and I straightened my shoulders, prepared for the clap back I know he was about to give.

"I ought to knock your teeth straight down the back of your throat," he said, as he grabbed hold of my face. I dared not flinch or show him I was intimidated by his usual antics.

We glared at each other for a few seconds more when he eventually released my face with a shove.

"You lucky I need to leave at this very moment, or I would have put your ass in check," he said to me before he turned to make his way out the kitchen.

"Maybe you should hire a maid, if you're not able to get out of your feelings to do shit around the house." I narrowed my eyes at him, as he gave me one final look before he left out of the kitchen.

I continued pecking at my bread as I heard the front door close shut, letting me know my husband had left. I shook my head as I continued flipping through the papers, not sure as to what I should make of my life.

So what could possibly have me all up in my feelings according to my husband? Well, it could be the fact that about three months ago he told me we would start a family. And of course, me being the naïve fool that I was, I believed him.

The only problem was that was nothing but bullshit. He never meant what he said about us starting a family. The only time we had sex was that very same day that he made the proposal to me; we never had sex again after that day.

Now call me crazy, but I do believe in order for me to get pregnant, I actually had to be fucking my husband!

I felt like the biggest fool in the whole world. Once again, my husband was able to make me look like an ass and he didn't even have to try very hard.

Clearly, I was nothing more than a joke to my husband, just a fucking plaything to him. He lifted my hopes having me believe he was finally ready to have a family with me.

The hardest part about all of this was the fact that I pushed King away. I hadn't seen or spoken to King for the past three months. I hadn't felt his touch, his kisses, his crazy Jamaican ways. I missed everything about him, I just wished there was some way I could reach out to him.

Honestly, I tried calling him on three separate occasions but of course, he never answered. I felt like one desperate woman but quite frankly, I could give a fuck. I missed the hell out of that man.

I was sure, on the other hand, that he wanted absolutely nothing to do with me, and who could blame him? The way he practically kicked me out of his home the last time we were together was almost embarrassing.

There was something about that day though that stuck with me. King had told me he couldn't wait for me to find out who I was really married to. I had no clue what he meant by that and of course I couldn't ask him, because he shut the door in my face.

I sighed as I flipped the page of the newspaper. As I was about to turn the page again, a story caught my attention.

Nightclub brawl leaves two people shot. I began reading the story as I pecked on my toast only to realize that this story was about King.

"What in the world," I whispered softly, as I placed the toast on my plate about to give this newspaper article my full attention.

Lifting the paper up in my hands, I began reading the story out loud.

"A fight at a popular nightclub has left two men nursing gunshot wounds and being hospitalized. An un-named source said that Kingsale Rock was in the company of a few of his friends, when another party-goer made a rude comment about the female he was with.

Sources say that Mr. Rock told the man to apologize to his woman, to which the man used profanity at Mr. Rock. It was at that time that Mr. Rock pulled out his firearm and proceeded to pistol whip the man. Not long after, the man's friends came to the rescue and a brawl broke out with over ten persons being involved.

Shots rang out leaving two people injured. One being the man Mr. Rock had the altercation with. Mr. Rock was taken in for questioning but was released because there was not enough evidence to charge him with anything. Mr. Rock was released from prison a few months ago after serving a two-year sentence for narcotics. Investigations are continuing."
I placed the paper down as I stared at the article.

The only thing that stuck out at me after I completed my reading, was who the fuck was King with? According to the story, he was with a woman. I was crazy jealous right about now.

I wondered who she was. Maybe it was the same chick I saw him with that day at the mall, the one who came with him to his sister's place for his welcome party.

I closed the newspaper and shoved it away from me. I was mad that I was mad! Because I had no right to be upset. I mean, what did I expect King to do? Did I honestly expect him to not move on after I blatantly told him I wanted nothing to do with him?

I sucked my teeth in annoyance as I stood up and discarded the remainder of my bread. I turned and made my way toward my bedroom with angry steps.

I was frustrated in more ways than one. My husband, no doubt, was up to his usual cheating ways again. My side piece had moved on with another bitch. And then here was my dumb ass all alone, with nobody to officially call my own.

I marched to my underwear drawer and opened it and shoved my hand to the back. I ran my fingers around until I found what I was looking for. I curled my lips in as I eyed the vibrator that became my new best friend over the last three months.

I closed and locked the bedroom door, removed my robe and under-wear and laid down on the bed. Spreading my legs apart, I turned the bullet on hearing the familiar buzzing sound. I wasted no time and placed my instrument of pleasure against my clit.

"Mmmmm," I groaned loudly, as the toy brought my body to life. I closed my eyes as King's faced appeared in my mind.

"Yeah, play with that fat pum pum," Imaginary King said to me as he stood and watched me pleasure myself.

"Use the other hand and rub on your nipples," Imaginary King instructed me, and I happily obliged. With one hand on my breast and the other between my thighs, I moaned in ecstasy as King watched me.

"That feel good baby?" he asked me.

"Yeah, yeah it does," I replied, as I circled my clit in a nice, slow movement.

"You miss your King, Sammie?" Imaginary King asked me.

"I miss you so much, can't you tell?" I replied as my movements sped up. I arched my back off the bed as I began feeling my orgasm building.

"Show me how much you miss me. Let me see you cum for your King; make that pussy cum for me Sammie."

With my head thrown back, and my back arched off the bed, I squeezed into my breast as I flicked my clit over and over again.

"Oh fuck, babyyyyy, King," I moaned shamelessly into the quiet bedroom as my body exploded into a million pieces. Beads of perspiration formed on my forehead as my body shook from my intense orgasm.

After a few seconds, I opened my eyes only to be greeted by an empty bedroom. Imaginary King was gone.

I shut my legs and switched the bullet off and smiled at myself. It honestly felt as though King was with me in that moment. I knew I had to see him. I could give a fuck if he didn't wish to see my face or not.

I missed my Jamaican King.

Selah

"**I**'m about to leave for work, Lamar," I said, as I grabbed my car keys up from off the dining table.

"You want me to drop you off?" Lamar asked, as he appeared in the living room, as I made my way to the front door. I rolled my eyes at his question because I didn't trust his ass for shit.

"Lamar, you left my ass stranded one too many times. I keep telling your ass I'll take myself to work from now on." I grabbed the knob and opened the door.

I felt his hand on my shoulder just as I walked out and I stopped to turn to him.

"Why have you been so grumpy lately?" he asked, as he eyed me up and down as he waited for my reply.

"I have not been grumpy," I said, in an angry tone.

"See, there you go right there. If this job is stressing you out, stay home. I got you." I honestly wanted to laugh in his face because if it wasn't for me, no bills would get paid up in this bitch. Lamar had been slacking so much lately with helping me out, I was this close to kicking his ass out of my house.

"Lamar, you and I both know that I need this job, so quit bugging. Look, I gotta go. I'll see you later." I reached in and gave him a quick kiss on his lips before I turned and walked off.

Climbing into my vehicle, I drove in silence to my work place. Truth

6

be told, I was on the verge of losing my mind. I often wondered if I should really be subjecting myself to this daily torture.

The last three months had been nothing short of a fucking nightmare. Jaime and I had not been on speaking terms, ever since I told him that we shouldn't be fooling around with each other. This nigga actually had the nerve to do what I said!

He hadn't made an attempt to touch me since. Our work relationship was exactly that…just work. His sister was also back so I didn't get to see him every day anymore, which was probably for the better.

The only thing was, I didn't like it one bit. Jaime barely looked at me when he spoke to me. If he did look my way, his expression was always blank and I could never read it. I didn't know if he felt like I was feeling, I didn't know if he missed me just as much as I missed him.

If he did feel the way I did, I couldn't tell because he was doing such an awesome job of hiding it from me. He was starting to irk my last nerve the way he'd been ignoring me. I wanted to march in his office and snatch him up by his shirt collar. Then shake him like a rag doll.

The day passed as it usually did; Jaime kept his sentences to me short and to the point, with hardly any eye contact. We were just going through the motions with me wishing that 5 o'clock would just hurry the fuck up.

When Jaime's final patient left for the day, he made his way inside of his office shutting his door quietly behind him as he did.

I chewed thoughtfully on the inside of my cheek as I stared at his closed door. Contemplating if I should go in and talk to him. I just wanted us to be able to have a normal conversation like we used to before.

I twisted my fingers nervously, deciding that I would just go on ahead and have a talk with Jaime. The front door to the business suddenly opened putting a pause on my plan. I could have sworn I had locked it after the last patient left.

I turned to the door and was about to let the person know that we were closed for the day. But my mouth immediately snapped shut, as my eyes fell on the female that stood at the front entrance.

This bitch was bad! My eyes roamed over her obviously very expensive designer, red and black work suit. Her skirt was very short and she wore a fitted jacket that hugged her petite frame. Her red pumps made her legs appear to have no end.

She wore her hair in a very low, platinum blonde haircut and her full, pouty lips were painted in a fire engine red. Her eyes looked me over as if she wasn't impressed by what she saw.

"I'm sorry, but we're closed for the afternoon," I told her, as I got up from behind my desk taking a couple steps closer to where she was standing.

Before she answered me, she made it her duty to allow her eyes to scan me slowly. From the tip of my toes, to the top of my head.

"I know you're closed. Can you tell Jaime, Yazmin is here," she said haughtily as she glowered at me.

My breath suddenly got caught in my chest when the realization hit me that she wasn't a patient. Rather, she was here to see Jaime...my Jaime!

"I'm sorry, was he expecting you? Because he never mentioned that he was expecting a visitor," I said, as I folded my arms across my chest.

The way her expression changed when she heard the term visitor, one would have sworn I called her mama a bad word.

"Excuse me, do I look like I came for a check-up to you? Do Jaime's patients normally come through dripping in Dolce and Gabbana? I don't think so, now can you please let him know *Yazmin* is here." She purposely stressed on her name as if I needed to hear it again.

I wanted to tell her just where she could stuff her Dolce and Gabbana outfit, but Jesus spoke to me just then and I remained quiet. Giving her a tight smile, I got up and walked to Jaime's office door.

Knocking twice, I gently turned the knob and opened the door. Jaime had his shirt off and was standing there with nothing but a plain white vest on. My heart missed a series of beats as he looked up at me.

"I'm sorry, I didn't know you were changing," I apologized to him as I forced my eyes to look away from his body.

"It's fine. I heard a voice. Is Yazmin out front?" I nodded my head letting him know that she was.

"Ok, let her know I'll be right out, I'm just changing my shirt." I couldn't help myself and looked over at him as he was shoving his arms inside of another shirt.

I wanted to ask him who the fuck was this Yazmin bitch and why did it obviously look as if he was about to take her out or some shit.

Instead, I just stood there staring at him, hoping he would stop acting as if we never shared anything intimate with each other.

"Did you want something else?" he asked, as he looked over at me as if I was bothering him.

With a wounded heart and pain filled eyes, I shook my head at him before closing the door. I kept my head lowered as I walked briskly back to my desk. Yazmin's eyes pierced a hole in my direction. I didn't have to look her way to know she was staring at me, I felt her eyes on me.

"He'll be right out," I mumbled to her, as I gathered up my belongings. Making sure as to never make any form of eye contact with her.

With my handbag slung over my shoulder, I hurried toward the front entrance.

"He's quite handsome isn't he?" Yazmin said, as I brushed past, but her words made my steps freeze as I looked at her.

"Excuse me?" I asked, making her smile.

"Jaime, he's handsome. I know you agree with me. I see the infatuation that you're trying to hide. I think it's…cute," she said, as she smirked at me. All I wanted to do at that very moment was slap that stupid grin off her face.

"I don't know what you mean," I said to her, as I glared into her face.

"Oh, you know exactly what I mean," she said, as she stepped closer to me. "Don't let this designer wear fool you; I can throw these hands if I want. Please make sure you and Jaime's relationship stays nothing more than being work related." I narrowed my eyes at her, thinking if punching her in her shit would be worth losing my job over.

I decided against it and turned to walk out the front door. The back of my neck burned with rage for a couple of reasons. The first being that Jaime was flaunting his new love interest in my face, which didn't sit well with me. The second reason being his new love interest seemed like a deranged bitch.

With my car keys in hand, I made my way to my vehicle in record time. Once inside, I exhaled a long, shaky breath as I started my car.

"Maybe I should just quit," I said inside of my quiet space as I pulled out of the parking lot making my way home.

I didn't want to admit it, but fucking my boss was a horrible fucking idea. All it got me was the most uncomfortable eight hours three days in every week.

Even though the dick was good, fucking great actually, it clearly was a mistake.

I cursed myself as I realized I took a wrong turnoff and signalled with my indicator to switch lanes. As I got in lane so that I could turn off at the next corner, I noticed a very familiar car about two cars ahead of me.

"Lamar," I said quizzically, as I wondered if I was seeing things. I sped up a little so that I could get a better view of the car and the license plate number. Sure enough, it was Lamar's vehicle. As I got closer to the corner I needed to turn off at, I realized he wasn't alone.

There was someone sitting in his passenger seat and from the looks of it, it was a female.

"I know this nigga is not cruising out here with another bitch," I said, just as I turned off at the corner. I wasted no time to pull my cell phone out and dial his number.

I called this fool a total of ten times and not once did Lamar answer my call. I was seeing stars as I drove fast as hell, wanting to make it home quickly so I could beat his ass.

I tried once more for the eleventh time and just as the other ten times, he never answered. So I decided to leave his ass a disrespectful voicemail.

"Lamar! I know you got me fucked up. Don't think I didn't just see your ass on the highway with some random bitch in your front seat! Acting like you don't wanna take my calls. I'mma fuck your ass up!" I screamed into my cell phone before tossing it on the seat next to me.

First Jaime, now Lamar. These niggas out here wildin'. I was about to set them both straight though, starting with Lamar's trifling ass!

King

I walked from out of my kitchen with a pack of frozen peas resting on my knuckles. My King pendant swinging from left to right against my naked stomach as I made my way over to my sofa.

My sweatpants hung under my ass as I sat down with a loud plop on my sofa. Resting my head to the sofa back, I inspected my bruised and sore knuckles, removing the peas pack.

I flexed my hand in and out making a fist, refusing to let the pain I felt from that movement faze me. The past three months had been nothing more than a blur to me. My behavior had been nothing short of being a lunatic.

I'd been high off weed and Hennessey almost every other night. I'd been getting into fights constantly for the stupidest reasons. In spite of all that, I had the most lucrative bunch of block boys selling my product.

However, I was fucked up all because of Samantha's stupid ass. I missed her way more than I thought I would but I refused to let my feelings get the best of me. Instead, I would buss a nigga's head all the way open, rather than admit or come to terms with the fact that I had possibly fallen in love with a married woman.

That was the reason why I'm nursing bruised knuckles right about now. A couple nights ago, me and my crew went out to a club, I met some random bitch there and we were chilling and kicking it. I promise that was the first time I ever saw that chick, so somebody please tell me why the fuck I got upset when a nigga said she had a fat punanny!

That wasn't my bitch but there I was asking the nigga to apologize to a bitch whose name I couldn't even remember. This was my behavior for the past three months…fucking reckless ass, Jamaican nigga.

In spite of the fact that I missed the fuck out of Sammie, she called me on three various occasions and I never once answered her call. I sat and watched that motherfucker ring. The palms of my hands were itching like crazy because I wanted to answer her call and tell her bring her stupid ass over here and let me love her. Instead, I had to man the fuck up and never answered her call.

Outside of being reckless by getting into fights every Friday night, I had been fucking the shit out of a few different women. Most of the time I barely even knew their first names. I know my momma probably looking down at me from heaven wanting to slap me upside my head.

There was a soft knock at the door and I looked at my wrist at the diamond encrusted Rolex. I tossed the peas to the side and got up to open my front door.

There stood one of my regular *bad gals*, Suzette. Or was it Stacy? I honestly couldn't remember at the moment.

"What you said your name was again?" I asked, as I ushered her inside. She got a look on her face that told me she was genuinely hurt by my question.

"Really Kingsale? I've been seeing you for more than a month now. My name is Tanya," she said, as she rolled her eyes at me.

Tanya, what the fuck? I was way off, I thought to myself as I admired her curvy body as her ass swayed from left to right in the short, sweat suit pants outfit she wore.

My dick began to rock up and I followed her to the sofa. Before she could even take a seat, I grabbed her hand and brought her down on top of my lap.

I roughly massaged her ass as she tried not to look as she was enjoying it. I'm guessing she was still pissed I didn't remember her name.

"Why don't you ever remember my name, Kingsale? I thought I meant something to you," she said, as she pouted her mouth in a dramatic way. I nearly laughed in her face because what made her think that she meant something to me?

"Don't worry about all of that. My dick missed the fuck out of you; go on ahead and give him a kiss," I told her, as I continued kneading into her ass.

She gave me a smile and I returned the gesture, glad that I was able to make her forget that I couldn't remember her name. Climbing off my lap, she got on her knees between my legs.

I eased my ass up off the sofa as I eagerly assisted her with pulling my sweats down. Giving her access to free my dick that desperately wanted to be freed.

"I love this big, Jamaican dick," Susan said, as she stroked my dick and licked her lips. *Wait a minute, was her name Susan?* A nigga was developing Alzheimer's, I swear.

"Let him feel your warm mouth, baby," I encouraged her as I placed my hand at the back of head, coaxing her head down.

I closed my eyes and bit into my lower lip as her mouth wrapped around my dick. I didn't wanna fuck, I just wanted to buss this nut down the back of her throat and kick her ass out my shit.

With that being my plan, I placed my hands at the side of her face and bobbed her head up and down, allowing her to try and take my full length down her throat.

"Look at me while I fuck your mouth baby," I said to her, and she did as she was told and looked up at me with her mouth full of my dick.

"Shit, make it extra wet," I instructed her just how I enjoyed getting my dick sucked. Taking her eyes off mine briefly, she applied a generous amount of saliva to the head of my dick and slurped loudly as I closed my eyes.

My phone began ringing to the side of me and I opened my eyes and peeped at the screen. *The fuck was this nigga calling me for?* I thought to myself as the name Taquan flashed on my screen.

I choose to ignore it as I concentrated instead on the head I was getting. Kathy was doing an alright job of sucking my dick but she wasn't the best, so I decided to hurry up and get this nut off so she could get the fuck out my house.

My phone began going off again and I sucked my teeth loudly.

Taquan's name flashed on my screen again and something told me I should take the call.

After the third ring, I grabbed up the phone in irritation and answered the call.

"Aye, *rudeboy*, the fuck you want nigga?" I answered rudely; the vibe of getting my dick sucked began to dissipate.

"Yo, we got a problem. Police done arrested the entire crew from off 8th Street." I sat up abruptly because this was the last thing I wanted to hear.

"The fuck, when the fuck did this happen!" I shouted into my cell. I roughly shoved what's-her-name away from me, as I adjusted my dick back inside of my sweatpants.

"About ten minutes ago. They took all them niggas down to the precinct. Shit don't look too good; they were all strapped and had their products on them." I scrubbed my face in agitation with the palms of my hand.

"Where are you now?" I asked Taquan, as I began putting my sneakers on my feet. I listened as Taquan gave me his location, and I got up from off the sofa as I ended the call and shoved the phone in my pocket.

I almost bumped into the chick whose name I was having a hard time remembering.

"What you still here? You need to bounce. I gotta be somewhere," I said, as I brushed past her, and she gasped in shock as I did so.

"You kicking me out Kingsale?" she asked in disbelief with both her eyebrows raised, as she stared at me.

"No, I'm not kicking you out. I'm telling you get out my shit but if you don't want to, then I'll be kicking you out," I explained myself calmly as I looked for my car keys for a new Escalade truck I bought recently.

She exhaled loudly in irritation as she stomped angrily toward the front door. Finally finding my keys, I followed her direction as I thought about the predicament I had to go deal with.

"Do me a favor and don't call me again," she said to me, just as she opened the door. I scrunched my face up at her wondering why she thought that would be a hard thing for me to do.

"Sonia, you ain't said nothing but a word; you ain't that special," I said, as I shook my head at her because she had a lot of fucking nerve.

"My name is Tanya, you fucking asshole!" she screamed at me, as I locked my front door and made my way to my vehicle. I waved her off, dismissing her correcting me for getting her name incorrect again. She jumped in her car and sped off.

As I pulled out of my driveway, I began counting the many times my niggas had gotten arrested for the last three months. I realized that every month at least two of my niggas from separate crews had gotten arrested.

That shit wasn't sitting right with me. I had been bailing niggas out of jail left to right. Not to mention I kept having to switch up their locations just to keep the police off their asses.

The more I thought about it, however, the more it started to feel like someone could be possibly targeting me. As I stopped at a red light, I swore a light bulb went off in my head.

"I know this *pussyhole* ain't the one fucking with me," I said to myself. Samantha's husband came to mind and my blood instantly grew hot because the more I thought about it, the more I was certain he was the one making all this shit happen.

He had enough connections to do this type of shit to me with his false ass. Out here pretending to be interested in doing good for his community meanwhile, he busy running his own drug blocks.

Since this nigga wanted to push me, I was prepared to push right back. I'd done my research and found out all the information I needed about Adam Daniel.

This nigga was about to be done fucking with my money. He was about to be taught a motherfucking lesson. The light turned green and I pulled off.

"That's why I was fucking your wife...you *battyboy*," I said, with a smile on my face as I thought about Samantha.

Adam Daniel

"I thought you said you were gonna divorce her before the end of the month Adam." I closed my eyes and exhaled softly as I tried to calm my nerves before I spoke.

I opened them and focused on Sandy Liverpool, the mother of my one-year-old twins. A boy named Alex and a girl named Alexandria.

"If you would just have some patience, I would file for a divorce soon, I promise." Sandy folded her arms tightly as she stood before me, glowering down at me in disapproval.

"I'm tired of your promises, Adam. We need you here with us. It's exhausting raising twins on my own, while you play dolly house with your wife," she said, as she turned and walked to sit at the opposite side of her living room.

"That's why I hired you the nanny, Sandy. So you could get all the help you need. What more do you want me to do?" I asked her with a shrug of my shoulders. Sandy rolled her eyes at me in a dramatic fashion before she looked away.

Well, I guess it's only fair that I confess how I met Sandy more than five years ago. It's no secret that I enjoy the company of women whose services I have to pay for. There was only one establishment I used when I wanted to enjoy my taste of exotic women. It was important that my identity remained a secret; the last thing I needed was for the public to know I was paying for pussy.

So for this reason, I stuck to only one escort business for providing me with the taste of women I preferred.

Anyway, I wanted to be in the company of a sexy, young female a few years back. I usually let all my escorts meet me at a particular hotel always in this one particular room.

I called up and requested my usual temptress named Amber, a blond haired, blue eyed bombshell. Only I was told that Amber was unavailable that night. The Madame then assured me that she had someone else that she was certain would make me just as happy as Amber, if not happier.

After a bit of reluctance on my end, she was finally able to persuade me to meet Sandy, who went by the name of Honeypot. Unfortunately, I had no idea that Sandy was new to her portfolio.

When she entered the hotel room that night, she took my breath away immediately. She had this nice, rich caramel complexion, with a body that had curves for days. Her hair was long and wavy that stopped mid-way down her back. She was so shy she could barely look me in my eyes.

So what did my stupid self do? I fell head over heels for Sandy. That night I didn't even touch her; we sat and talked for hours getting to know each other better. I found out that Sandy lived with her older brother, Samuel. Her mother was an absentee mom, hardly ever at home with her two kids. Her father was shot and killed when she was only six years old.

Her brother practically brought them both up but of course, her brother belonged to the streets. He was heavy in the drug game, so heavy that he introduced Sandy to the street life as well. She told me her brother would use her as a decoy to help him set up niggas; she was also used to drop off drugs to buyers.

She said she did most of the work but her brother kept majority of the profits.

Her breaking point came when she was almost gang raped when she was given a duffel bag full of marijuana and cocaine to drop off at an abandoned warehouse. She told her brother she wanted out but all that got her was a whopping.

Desperate to start making her own money, she got introduced to a different type of fast life…being an escort.

She had been doing this job for only about a month when she met me.

17

After she told me her story, I decided to play *captain save a hoe* and promised her that I would help her out, and I did.

I MOVED her out of her apartment that she shared with her brother, one of those section 8 apartments. She now lived in an upscale part of town in her own fully furnished, three-bedroom home.

Since I started messing with Sandy, I rarely used the escort service anymore. Occasionally, I would take a taste every now and again, but not as frequently as I used to.

Then she became pregnant and I almost shit my appendix out when she said she was keeping her baby. I tried unsuccessfully to convince her why it was a fucking awful idea to follow through with the pregnancy, but it fell on deaf ears.

Those nine months were hard as fuck getting her to doctor's appointments without anything being traced back to me. I obviously couldn't accompany her to any which always ended up with us getting into an argument because she wanted me to be present at her check-ups.

Things worked out though and I got the most beautiful mixed twins I ever laid my eyes on. I loved my kids with my all, but I for fucks sake didn't want anymore. That's why I had a vasectomy a few months after they were born.

I never told anyone a motherfucking thing, kept that little fun fact to myself. I knew I was probably a fucked up nigga for breathing false hope at Samantha, making her believe we could someday have a baby.

I decided that when the time came I would make up a story saying the doctor said I had a low sperm count. Then I would just convince her that we should adopt, shouldn't be too hard.

"I don't want a nanny, Adam. I want my man!" she yelled at me, as she stomped her feet in defiance. "You always choose her over us and I'm sick of it. You keep promising that you'll divorce her and you never do. You claim you don't love her but your actions speak volumes," Sandy said, as she scooted to the edge of the sofa as she pointed her index finger at me.

"Sandy, let's not do this not tonight. I'm not tryna argue with you.

Besides, you'll wake the twins up." Sandy gave me a deathly stare as if she thought staring at me like that would have turned me to stone.

I was about to reassure her that I would get a divorce in the near future when my phone began ringing in my pants pocket. Glad for the interruption, I fished the phone out quickly and watched the screen. I smiled to myself.

"Talk to me," I said, as I answered the call.

"I did what you asked me to do. We arrested his entire crew a short while ago." I smiled as those words filled my ear.

"Good, try to get as much charges you could bring against them," I instructed, as I stood up deciding that I should make my way home.

"What about the payment? When can I expect it?" I swear in this city, money could buy even the most loyal of police officers.

"Don't worry, I got you. I'll swing by your office and handle that for you tomorrow," I said, before we said our goodbyes and I hung up the phone.

I turned around to face a scowling Sandy. I cursed myself silently because she was starting to ride my last nerve.

"Where you about to go?" she asked me, as she snapped her neck back and forth. I hated when she acted like she was from the projects, shit was so unappealing to me.

"Chill out with all that turkey neck bullshit. I'll be back tomorrow," I said, as I made my way toward the front door. I felt her hand grab me roughly and I had to force myself not to deck her straight in her face.

"Don't be pulling on me like that, Sandy! Fuck is wrong with you?" I asked her, as I spun angrily around to face her. This got her attention and she immediately let go of my arm.

"Take your ass back in the house and see about my kids. Like I said, I'll swing by tomorrow. I got somewhere I need to be." Without giving her so much as a second look, I walked out the house toward my parked car.

As I climbed inside, I smiled to myself. King was in for a rude awakening; this lil' young nigga thought he had something on me. He was gonna learn that I'm not one to be fucked with.

I pulled out into the street about to make my way home. I felt real proud of myself right about now. Bit by bit I was going to watch King fall to his knees.

I was about to take back my streets and dethrone that young nigga… the streets were about to be mine again.

Samantha

J had no idea what the fuck I was even doing and if this was even a good idea.

I squeezed the steering wheel as I drove toward Kwana's apartment. I came up with this plan since King didn't wish to take my calls. I was going to trick his ass into meeting me.

Poor Kwana, I roped her into what I came up with and she agreed to have King come over to her house and I would show up and prayed and hoped that all went well from there.

I pulled up in front of the apartment building and cut the engine off. I parked directly behind what looked like a new Escalade truck, which could have only belonged to King. I checked my appearance in the rear-view mirror; my make-up was very light with a nude colored lipstick on my lips.

My hair had soft curls that framed my face. I looked down at my short fitted, denim dress that I wore with wedge heel shoes. I exhaled loudly in my car and decided it was now or never.

I climbed out and made my way to the front entrance, the usual dope hustlers standing to the front of the building as I passed them. I felt their eyes on me but I paid them no mind because the person I was really interested in was King.

I walked up to Kwana's door and knocked on it gently. I stood and waited patiently for the door to open.

Kwana opened up and rolled her eyes before looking back into the apartment as if she was being followed. Shoving her way out, she closed the door behind her.

"Hey, Kwana," I said, as I leaned in and gave her a hug.

"I hope you know just what I'm doing for you here. When King finds out that I set this up, he's gonna kill my ass," Kwana said, as she moved away from me and folded her arms as she looked at me.

"I know, and I really do appreciate you doing this but girl, your brother is so hard headed he refuses to take any of my calls," I said, in a pleading type of voice. Kwana shook her head at me.

"What's he doing?" I asked, not thinking I could wait any longer to see him.

"He's in the shower. I told him he should come go with Kaden and me to the park," Kwana said, as she placed her hand on the door knob as she began to turn it.

"Let me grab Kaden and we can go before my crazy brother gets out of the bathroom." I stood in silence as she retreated into her bedroom and returned with a smiling Kaden in her arms.

My heart instantly melted at the sight of him and I reached out and ran my fingertips across his chubby cheeks.

"Hey there, Kaden," I said, in a sing-song manner. He began talking in baby gibberish as drool ran down his chin.

"Ok, we about to dip. Good luck with my big-headed brother girl, you'll need it," Kwana said, as she made her way toward the door.

"Thanks again for this," I told her as I walked with her.

"Thanks nothing, sis, you better have my back when King tries to murder my ass," she said, as she walked out the door with Kaden on her hip.

I closed the door behind her and turned to the sound of the bathroom door being opened and then closed.

King emerged with a towel draped around his waist and one over his head as he towel dried his hair.

His hand rubbed vigorously on his head, his vision obscured allowing me to take in the man that I missed over the last three months.

His firm chest glistened with water droplets, his arms with all his tattoos looked as if he added a few muscles on there. His outlined stomach was begging me to dig my nails into it as I'd done so many times when he was laying his pipe on me.

And the wonderful dick print that was hidden under his towel, bobbed left and right from his hand movements. My mouth salivated at the sight of this sexy Jamaican God.

"Kwana!" he shouted, just as he removed the towel from off his head. My breath caught in my throat as his eyes scanned the room before they fell on me standing by the door.

We could do nothing but stand and stare at each other, the seconds felt like hours.

"What the fuck are you doing here? Where's Kwana and Kaden?" he asked, as his expression turned ice cold.

"They left," I managed to say softly, and he got a very confused look on his face.

"Left? Kwana!" he shouted out again as he walked back in the direction of the bedrooms. I stood and waited for him to do his security sweep before he realized that it was just us two in the apartment.

"What the fuck is this? Where did Kwana go so I could find her and kill her stupid ass?" King said, as he came stomping back into the living room.

"I wanted to see you, King. So she helped me set this up. I really missed you," I said, as I waited for him to say something.

"Why you even here, shouldn't you be pregnant by now?" I became slightly annoyed that he completely ignored the fact that I just told him that I missed him.

"I'm here because I needed to see you, King, and I'm not pregnant," I told him, as I shyly looked down at my feet.

"OK, well you can leave now," he said, as he pointed at the door behind me. I screamed in my head because he was so hard headed and he wasn't about to make this easy for me.

"No, King, I'm not about to leave. I want us to talk. Can't you talk to me?" I said, knowing damn well I was probably sounding very desperate, but I didn't care at this point.

"Talk about what, Sammie? Didn't you make your choice, didn't you say you were gonna start a family and that I was too young for you? And that it would never work out between us? So tell me again what the fuck you wanna talk about," I could hear the malice and hate in his voice and I began re-thinking this visit.

"I made a mistake, it's just I really wanted to start a family and I thought that Adam was finally going to give our marriage a try. But it was all just bullshit; he's back to his usual tricks again…and I miss you so much," I said, as I closed the space between us.

We were now standing facing each other. I saw King's eyes sweep admiringly over my body and for a split second, I saw the yearning in his eyes. It disappeared just as quickly as it appeared though, replaced with his icy cold glare.

"Aight bet, you done?" Whatever glimmer of hope I had for this visit to work out in my favor went right down the toilet by the way he was acting. I began feeling silly for thinking this would have worked out.

"Just forget it, if you're gonna be such an asshole," I mumbled under my breath as I spun around to get back into my car so I could feel embarrassed in private.

"An asshole," I heard him say as he followed my steps. "You made your choice Sammie, you chose to stay with your *pussyhole* husband. Don't come at me with this bullshit because you all of a sudden realized you made the wrong choice, with yo' stupid ass."

Ignoring his words, I grabbed the doorknob and pulled the door open only to have King shut it from his position behind me. Feeling defeated, I kept my back to him as I felt his body heat from where we stood.

"I didn't mean to upset you, King. I just thought that maybe you missed me just as much as I missed you, but I see now that I was wrong," I said softly, as I exhaled in frustration.

"Guess you thought wrong," King said in my ear. I believed I'd had enough of his antics and decided that I should just leave.

"I guess so, back up so I can leave then," I said as I took a step backward only to be pressed into his firm body. I gasped as I felt his hard dick stick me in my lower back.

I smiled to myself because at least I knew I still had some kind of effect on him. I turned around slowly to face him and I saw nothing but pure, raw lust in his eyes. I looked down at his erection and the way it stuck out from under his towel.

"Don't let this hard dick fool you, I don't want nothing to do with your ass," he said, as he turned and walked away from me. He sat down on the sofa and it was as if my legs had a mind of their own. I walked over and sat next to him.

"Don't you miss me, don't you miss us?" I asked as I brushed my fingers against his exposed arm. King turned to me, his eyes drinking in my lips and I was convinced that he was about to give in...I was wrong.

"I think you should leave," he said, as he pulled his arm away from me.

"Fine!" I yelled as I shoved his arm in rage and got up from off the sofa.

"I ought to drop you on your ass for putting your hands on me like that, Sammie," King said, as he got up from out his seat as I did.

I folded my arms tightly across my chest as we stood face to face once again.

"All I was trying to do was let you know I missed you and that I was sorry for how I acted, but you're being a dick about this." Let me just say this, the next turn of events made this visit go downhill real quick.

King decided that he needed to unwrap the towel he had around his waist and place it around his neck instead. I gave him a very confused look as my eyes travelled down his naked body, his dick standing at attention.

"Well it's not gonna suck itself," he said calmly.

Embarrassed was not a big enough word for how I felt to what King was insinuating.

"Fuck you, King," I spat at him, but all that got me was a laugh in my face.

"I thought you said you missed me though." He continued to chuckle as he wrapped the towel back around his waist. I had officially had enough of his shenanigans.

"Fuck you, King," I said to him once more as I roughly shoved him on his chest as hard as I could. I spun on my feet to make my exit.

"Na, fuck you, Sammie. You made your choice to be with your *battyboy* husband, don't get mad now. And what I tell you 'bout putting your hands on me like that?" I heard his footsteps behind me as I made it to the front door and pulled it open.

"Next time, come prepared to suck my dick," I heard him say just as I walked out the front door. My face was hot with shame as I opened my car door and sat in the driver's seat.

I couldn't believe the way King acted but then again, I shouldn't blame him. I brought this upon myself.

I exhaled loudly and closed my eyes for a brief second. I guess it was safe to say that King and I were officially over!

Selah

ell this was fucking embarrassing, I thought to myself as I walked down the aisle of the pharmacy.

My life had been nothing short of a movie this past week. First, I kicked Lamar's ass out of my house; good riddance to that motherfucker.

I confronted his ass that day I saw him driving down the highway with some chick in his front seat. And just like the true man he was, he denied that shit with a straight face.

This fool swore up and down that it wasn't his car that I saw, until I told him I looked directly at his number plate. Now how many vehicles driving around with the exact same plates?

Then this stupid motherfucker changed his tune real quick, talking 'bout he was giving his homeboy's girl a lift to a hair salon where she had made her appointment.

Was I really supposed to believe that story?

But that wasn't even the real reason why I kicked his ass out my house. So yesterday, I'm at work and my pussy began feeling as though some alien had taken it over.

I raced to the bathroom, pulled my underwear down and I swore something done crawled up my pussy and died. I had an odor and a gray and yellow discharge on my Kotex panty shield.

As if that wasn't enough, I was experiencing pain whenever I urinated; this shit was bad.

I knew something was most definitely wrong with me. Thank goodness that day I worked with Mrs. Smith and not Jaime. After she was done with her last patient and we were wrapping up for the day, I went to her office door and knocked on it.

"Hey Selah, you ready to call it a day?" she asked me as I entered, catching her in the middle of tidying up her desk.

I stepped inside of her office and twisted my fingers, feeling nervous about asking what I was about to.

"Is everything OK?" she asked me. I'm guessing she saw the uncertainty in my face.

"Actually no, do you think you can give me a check-up right quick?" I knitted my eyebrows together as I looked up at her.

With a concerned expression on her face she said, "Of course I can. What's happening with you?" She took a few steps to me.

"I've been having a discharge and pain when I urinate and I have somewhat of an odor," I explained, feeling mortified hearing those words pass my lips, even though I knew Mrs. Smith probably heard this often from her patients.

"No problem, go on over to the examination room and lay down. I'll be with you shortly." I thanked her and left her office anticipating this check-up so I could know exactly what was happening to me.

"OK, I'm all done, Selah," Mrs. Smith said, about ten minutes after I laid down on her examination table.

"Do you know what's happening with me?" I asked, as I sat upright waiting for her diagnosis.

"You have what's called Trichomoniasis." *Oh Jesus*, I was fucking dying.

"Oh my god, is that fatal? I'm dying, aren't I?" I asked, feeling as though I was about to burst into tears. I covered my face with my hands.

"No, no, no. Relax Selah, it's not fatal. Trichomoniasis is caused by a protozoan organism, nothing a week of antibiotics won't cure," Mrs. Smith said as she smiled at me. I breathed an exaggerated sigh of relief.

"How does one get *Trichowhatever*?" I enquired, as I got up from off the examining table to get dressed.

"Um, did you change sex partners recently? Trichomoniasis is a very common STI." I stopped and looked her way. *Oh hell nah*, a STI. Of course I wasn't about to blurt out that I fucked her family so I shook my head no.

"Well if you didn't, then unfortunately your boyfriend did. Consider using condoms when you guys are being intimate. Meet me in my office for the prescription." With those being her final words, she left out of the examination room leaving me seeing red.

Lamar, that dirty dick motherfucker, gave me an infection. I was about to kill his motherfucking ass! I knew it had to be him. Seeing how Jaime and I had sex over three months ago, it couldn't have been him.

Plus, I remembered him saying he got a regular check-up often. So it was safe to say my man gave me an STI.

So here I was about to get this medication for my pussy a day after in the pharmacy. I walked up to the counter and handed the lady the prescription.

"Can you tell me if y'all got this please?" I said, as she took the paper from out my hand. She looked at the prescription and seemed unsure of something by the look on her face.

"Hold on, let me ask the pharmacist," she said as she excused herself and walked to the back. "Yazmin, do we have this?" I heard her ask.

I stood in absolute shock as the pharmacist appeared and took the paper from out of her hand. *Fuck my life*, I thought as Jaime's love interest read the words of the prescription and looked over to where I was standing.

I must have done something really wrong in my past life for this to be happening to me right now. Yazmin recognized me right away and walked over to where I was standing behind the counter.

"Selah, is it?" she asked, as she looked at me with my prescription in her hand.

"Yes, and you're Yazmin, right?" I played along with her as I gave her a slight smile.

"Cute because I know you remember my name," she said, as she waved my prescription around.

"Do you have what I came here for? I'm in kind of a hurry," I told her because she was starting to get on my nerves already, and she just now showed up.

"Yes we do, let me hurry up and get this for you. I know you probably need it urgently for your little problem," she replied, as she averted her eyes downward at my crotch.

I swear I would reach over this counter so that I could grab her and beat her ass. I didn't even know why she had an issue with me; she must be one insecure chick.

Turning around, she went to see about filling my prescription as I stood and waited in silence.

A few minutes later, she came back with my medication and handed it to me with a wide smile on her face.

"You pay up front," she told me. I snatched my medication from out of her reach and turned to walk away. But Yazmin just had to have the last say.

"I'll be sure to let Jaime know you stopped by." Without thinking twice, I marched right back to the counter.

"I do believe there's such a thing as customer confidentiality. Don't get fucked up," I said through gritted teeth as I threatened her.

Obviously not one to be intimidated easily, Yazmin bent her body to get closer to me.

"What you need to do is go see about your infected pussy." I narrowed my eyes at her before I turned and walked off.

If I stood there any longer, I was pretty sure I would end up in a jail cell before the day was out.

A bitch didn't feel like going to prison today.

King

Man to man is so unjust, children ya don't know who to
   trust,
Your worst enemy could be your best friend,
And your best friend your worst enemy.

I pulled on my blunt as I sang along with my nigga Bob Marley as I drove to my destination. This visit would end either two ways, bad or very fucking bad; either way, I was prepared for the outcome.

As I drove and listened to my music and smoked this good ass kush, my mind wandered back to Sammie and her little visit she paid me the other day.

I smiled at the thought and shook my head. A nigga felt kind of happy that she missed me as much as she did to trick a nigga into seeing her.

Even though I was glad to see her after so long, I wasn't about to act like it…fuck no! So I decided to fuck with Sammie a little and not give in. The fuck she thought, that I was going to make shit easy for her?

I had to show her stupid ass that she had to deal with the consequences of choosing a nigga who was as fake as those females' ass from *Love and Hip Hop*.

Speaking of that nigga, I pulled up in front of Sammie's husband's work place. I switched my engine off and continued smoking the last of my weed.

I opened the door and hopped out, tossing the last of my blunt at my feet and stomping on it. I then walked casually to the entrance. As I was about to open the front door, it opened for me and a lady stepped out almost crashing into me.

"I'm sorry," she said as she looked up at me, and I recognized her instantly.

This was the chick from when I drove Adam over to her house that one time; Sandy I believe her name was. The very chick I first had any encounter with over at my sister's apartment.

I could tell she realized who I was by the way her expression changed. She tried to walk by me but I rudely stood in her way.

"Don't I know you?" I asked her, as I looked her up and down.

"No, I think you have the wrong person, sorry," she said, as she tried to walk by me again.

"Girl, why you lying? I dropped your ass home that one time when you were over at my sister Kwana's apartment," I told her, as if I really needed to explain shit to her.

"Oh yeah, I remember now." I gave her a look, letting her know she was on some bullshit. I decided to pry a little by asking her a question.

"You work here?" I asked her, as I pointed to the building.

"No, but my man does. Now if you'll excuse me, I'm late." Moving out of her way, I smiled to myself because I knew she was talking about Adam. That little bit of information she just shared could be useful in a few minutes. I continued walking into the building and made my way to the receptionist, who was sitting gnawing away on her gum like some damn Billy goat. Her rude ass didn't even bother to look up as I stood at the desk.

"Aye, is Mr. Daniel in office today?" I said, as I knocked the desk loudly, forcing her to look up at me. She gave me a rude look from behind her glasses, as if I was aggravating her to do the job she was paid to do.

"I know you're not speaking to me." *The fuck*, I thought to myself as I gave her a pissed off look. I looked to the back from where she sat and saw a closed door that read "Councillor Adam Daniel" on it.

I don't know why she thought I needed her approval. Not giving her so much as a second look, I walked past her and made my way to the door.

"Excuse me, you can't go in there," I heard her say, as I pushed the door open. Adam was on his cell phone and he looked up as I barged into his office.

"I'm so sorry Mr. Daniel, he just walked in without permission," the receptionist apologized as if she was scared she would be fired.

"It's OK, Jessica, I was expecting him," Adam said as he ended his call. I looked over at Jessica and smiled, waving her off. She gave me a cold, evil glare before she exited the office, shutting the door loudly behind her.

I chuckled at her, loving the way I got under her skin. Without being told to, I sat down in the chair opposite Adam and got comfortable as he stared angrily at me.

"What the fuck are you doing here? This is my place of business," he said, as he interlocked his fingers that sat on top of his desk, as he waited for my reply.

"You know why I'm here nigga. Stop fucking with my crew, stop sending those dirty ass cops to arrest my niggas. I know it's you doing that shit and I would like you to bring an end to it," I said calmly as I ran the palm of my hand on my beard that needed to be trimmed.

"I don't believe I know what you're talking about. If anyone you know was arrested I'm sure the police had good reason to carry out their duties," Adam said with a smirk on his face.

"Yo, you think I'm playing with you. You want to make as much money as me and my niggas are making, then get with the right grade of marijuana. You stay selling that weak shit. Get with the Jamaican high grade; I'll sell it to you for a good price." It was my turn to smirk at him but he got real serious.

"You think you intimidate me, you lil' Jamaican hooligan." I didn't particularly like his tone and it was time for me to let him know exactly where I was coming from.

"You can call me all the names you wanna call me Big D," I said, calling him by his street name which got his attention because he sat upright in his seat as he glared at me.

"Yeah, I know all about you; I did my research. I found out all there is to know about you and your illegal drug blocks. And if you don't want everyone finding out exactly who their beloved councillor really is, ease up off me and my crew *rudeboy*," I said, allowing my accent to sound really thick.

"I think it's time you left," Adam said, as he slid his chair back, giving the assumption he was about to get up and do something.

"Oh yeah, you might want to be careful about having your mistress parading in and out of your office. We wouldn't want that information getting out to the public either." I smiled at him as I got up from out my seat to make my exit.

"I refuse to let you get under my skin. Now get the fuck out my office...*King*." This nigga said my name as if it were a dirty word. I stopped walking to look his way.

"You just remember what I said. You don't want these problems from a Jamaican shotta like myself," I said, as I tapped my chest loudly. "The last thing you want is to see your empire crumble at your feet." I looked around his office so he would know exactly where I was coming from. I gave him one last sinister stare before I opened the door.

Realizing that I still had some asshole left in me, I turned to him as I walked through the doorway.

"How's Sammie, doing? Tell her King said hey." I saw the confused expression that crept on his face and I gave him a devilish smile before I left out his office.

I passed the disgruntled receptionist on my way out and blew a kiss at her, which only made her turn her nose up at me. I walked coolly outside to my Escalade and hopped in.

The music of Bob Marley filled the inside of my ride again as I pulled out of the parking lot. My cell phone began ringing in my pocket and I took it out and looked at the screen.

I contorted my face in confusion because this number was out of state and I didn't recognize it. I slid my finger across the screen and answered the call.

"Yo, who this?" I asked, as I waited for the caller to identify themselves.

"Kingsale, *what ah gwan my youth*?" a heavy Jamaican accent said on the other end. I removed the phone from my ear and watched the screen again as if that would somehow help me figure out who the fuck was on the phone.

"Who's this?" I asked again.

"It's your cousin, Mark. I was calling to let you know Uncle Joseph had a heart attack." I almost crashed my motherfucking ride hearing that shit. I pulled to the side of the road as I waited for the rest of the information fearing the worst.

"Is he ok, Mark?" I asked, as I held my breath. I mean, my uncle and I had our differences, but I didn't want to hear nothing happened to him, especially so soon after my mother's passing.

"The doctors say he'll pull through but he's been asking to see you. I think you should come home for a visit." I shut my eyes as I tried to process what he said. This timing was definitely not the best for me to travel to Jamaica. I needed to be here and guard my business from Sammie's husband.

"Yo, Mark, I don't think that's a good idea me coming out there right now," I said softly, not enjoying that I was denying visiting my ailing uncle.

"My youth, I think you should re-think ya words. If something happens to Uncle Joseph, think about how you'll feel." I closed my eyes again and exhaled softly because he was right.

"Aight, I'll start looking at flights and let you know how soon I'll be there."

"Looking forward to seeing you; it's been a while *my youth*." My cousin and I talked for a couple minutes more before I ended the call.

Not giving it much thought after hanging up the phone with Mark, I dialed a number and waited for the call to be answered.

"What you want big head?" Kwana answered rudely, making me regret I even called her ass.

"Shut up, you should be nice to me after that stunt you and Sammie pulled the other day," I said to her, as I pulled my car out from the side of the road and continued driving.

"What do you want King?" she asked, as if I was some type of nuisance to her.

"Do Kaden have his passport? We about to take a trip home to Jamaica."

Selah

*T*his was some bullshit.

I pulled out a few wet wipes as I hoisted my leg on the toilet seat so that I could give my pussy a whore's bath.

Ever since I was diagnosed with contracting a STI a few days ago, this had been my daily routine. I turned into a clean freak, always sneaking away as often as I could to deal with my hygiene.

I no longer had an odor and my discharge was almost completely gone. Every time I looked at my pussy, I cursed that dirty dick mother-fucker Lamar in my head.

I told him he infected me and of course he denied that also, just like he did about the female I saw in his car. I swear I couldn't stand his ass, don't know why I wasted my time dating him in the first place.

I tossed the wipes in the toilet and flushed them down. I adjusted my work skirt that I knew damn well was too short and fixed my shirt that was tucked neatly inside my skirt.

Today I was working with Jaime, so how I looked was important as fuck. I walked out and stood by the sink as I washed my hands. Looking in the mirror, I flipped my freshly braided, butt-length box braids over my shoulder. I knew Jaime told me that one time we had sex that he enjoyed grabbing them, so I always made sure I wore my hair like this.

We had one more patient for the day which was that loud mouth chick,

Shantel Cudjoe. I really couldn't stand her ass and I couldn't wait for her visit to be over and done with.

Shantel was now six months pregnant and had to come to get her check-ups on a monthly basis. We never got to meet her baby's father, who she bragged about all the time. She swore that he was paid and couldn't wait to spoil his baby.

Jaime was convinced that the father was no longer in their lives and that Shantel was just putting up a front. Whatever it was, I just wanted her visit to be over with so her loud ass could be on her way.

I made my way from out of the bathroom at the very same time Shantel was walking through the office front door.

"Hey girl," she said, way too loud as if I was standing in another state and not a couple feet away from her.

"Hi, Shantel," I replied to her greeting, giving her a smile. She actually looked well put together today. She wore a loose fitted maxi dress that stopped at her ankles, with a pair of sandals on her feet. Her lace-front wig was in a high ponytail and she wore a ridiculous amount of make-up on her face.

"I'm ready to push this baby out. I'm as big as a house," she said, as she rubbed her pregnant stomach. I smiled with adoration at her protruding belly, wishing one day I could experience the joy of pregnancy. I mean, I was thirty-six years old, my biological clock was ticking.

"Why don't you have a seat and let me get Mr. Francis." I waited for Shantel to be seated before I made my way to Jaime's office.

I knocked on the door before entering only to find Jaime standing with his back to me, looking out the only window in his office, staring off in space. He was so lost in his own world he had no idea I had entered so I used this opportunity to admire him.

His hands were shoved in his pants pocket, and his ass looked superb in his work pants. His shirt hugged his broad shoulders, those shoulders that I grabbed and dug my nails into when he drove his dick inside of me.

Ok, my thoughts were definitely straying. I cleared my throat loudly and he finally realized he wasn't alone. With a startled look on his face, he spun around to face me.

The first thing I noticed as he turned to me was the massive bulge in his pants. I couldn't help but gawk at his obvious erection. Whoever Jaime had been fantasying about as he gazed out that window, sure had an effect on him.

Clearing his throat, he ducked behind his chair as if I didn't already see that his dick was hard. I suddenly felt a bit jealous because I was sure he'd probably been thinking about Yazmin's stuck up ass.

"Um, your last patient for the day is here," I said to him, and he simply nodded his head at me.

"Have her wait for me in the examination room, I'll be right there," Jaime said, as he kept the bottom half of his body hidden behind the chair.

"Sure, I see you need some time to get yourself together." I averted my eyes at his crotch so that he could catch my meaning.

I closed the door behind me as I walked to Shantel and led her into the examination room.

Roughly fifteen minutes later, we all stared at the screen at the peanut sized fetus that was sucking its thumb.

"Aww, look at my lil' man," Shantel cooed, as she looked at her baby on the monitor. I smiled along with her as I watched her baby; she found out she was having a boy at her last visit.

"Do you have any names as yet?" Jaime asked her, as he wiped the ultrasound gel from off her stomach.

"Yes, I'm going to name him after his daddy," Shantel replied, bursting with pride. Jaime and I exchanged our secret glance at each other. Because Shantel always talked so highly of the father who never once showed up at any of her appointments.

"Well I guess the baby's name is going to be Casper then," Jaime cracked with reference to Casper the ghost being her baby daddy.

"You ain't funny doc," Shantel said, as she got up from off the table and started to get dressed. "My baby is going to be named Lamar Richards Jr. after his daddy." I froze at what she said; my eyes growing the size of lemons.

"Lamar Richards? That's your baby father's name?" I asked, as I looked at her with my mouth opened. I knew this had to be a joke; she couldn't possibly be talking about the same Lamar.

"Yeah girl, why?" she asked as she eyed me with curiosity as she waited for my answer.

Still finding it hard to believe that Lamar had fathered a whole baby behind my back, I described Lamar to Shantel, every last detail of his appearance.

"Yes, that's him. How do you know my baby daddy?" Shantel asked, as she folded her arms above her huge, milk filled boobs. She narrowed her eyes in menacing slits at me.

I suddenly felt as though my shirt was too tight, the ceiling was coming down on the top of my head and that I couldn't breathe.

I looked over in Jaime's direction and he had a look on his face that said he placed two and two together.

Knowing that I needed to get away from that examination room, I excused myself and bolted out the door in the direction of the bathroom.

Once inside, I locked the door behind me and stood in front of the sink just in time as I felt the bile rising in my throat. I bent over and puked my guts out as warm tears rolled down my cheeks.

This was a motherfucking nightmare. I felt like my life had been falling apart a little more every day.

What did I do to deserve all the bullshit Lamar had put me through? I mean, I knew we weren't together anymore, but that didn't mean this shit didn't hurt. He fathered that baby when we were still very much in a relationship.

I guess that's why he never bothered showing up at any of her appointments. I mean, how clueless could one person be? Didn't he think that his big mouth baby momma would not have mentioned his name at some point?

I stayed my ass in that bathroom for almost twenty minutes before a soft knock came at the door.

"Selah," Jaime called out to me. I shut my eyes for a quick second and opened them to look at my reflection in the mirror. I looked a hot mess. Opening the faucet, I splashed some water on my face as I tried to get it together.

With a deep breath, I walked to the door and opened it. Jaime stood with a very concerned look on his face.

"Hey, are you alright?" he asked, with genuine concern in his eyes. Plastering a big, fake smile on my lips, I nodded my head at him letting him know I was OK.

I brushed past him as I went to my desk to gather up my things.

Because quite frankly, I'd had enough of this day. There was no need to ask if Shantel had left because I hid in that bathroom long enough, giving her sufficient time to leave.

"I guess I'll see you tomorrow," I said, trying not to make any kind of eye contact with him because I was embarrassed to do so.

"Selah," Jaime said, as he came to me and placed his hands on my upper arm, forcing my movements to stop. "I'm sorry you had to find out like that." I still couldn't bring myself to look directly in his eyes so I kept my eyes on my black pumps on my feet.

"I really shouldn't even be mad really. I broke up with Lamar a few days ago but he impregnated Shantel when we were supposed to be in a relationship. I can't understand what I did to deserve this," I said, hating the fact that I sounded as if I was feeling sorry for myself.

"Don't do that Selah, don't think that this was your fault. You're a beautiful Queen that deserves nothing but the best. It's his loss for not realizing what he had," Jaime said, as he tilted my head up by holding me by my chin, forcing me to look at him.

"Any man would be lucky to have you in his life. I mean that, Selah." Jaime's eyes fell on my lips and I wanted nothing more than to feel this man's mouth all over my body.

Before either of us could change our minds, our lips touched in a sensual kiss. Using the tip of his tongue, Jaime coaxed my mouth open which I was more than happy to let him in.

Our tongues did some type of weird tongue ritual dance as they entwined with each other's. I moaned into Jaime's mouth as I felt him wrap his hand around my braids and tug my head further back.

"I fucking missed your ass," Jaime said, as he bit into my lower lip causing me to groan even louder.

Jaime backed us up until my ass was pressed against the edge of my desk. His hand began inching its way under my skirt and that's when a red light flashed in my mind.

I had totally forgotten that my pussy wasn't 100% yet. I was about to push his hand away as it neared my underwear when his cell phone began to ring.

I breathed a sigh of relief as Jaime moved away from me uttering curse words under his breath.

"Hello," he said, as he took his call. I adjusted my clothing as I eavesdropped on his call. From the way he spoke, I knew he was talking to Yazmin and I rolled my eyes as I gathered my belongings.

"Yeah come on in," he said to her as I picked my car keys up from my desk. Jaime turned to me as I began to walk toward the front door.

"By the way, I sent you an email while you were in the bathroom earlier," he said, as he touched his lips with his fingers.

"An email, about what?" I asked, as I paused just as I reached the door.

"We have another conference to attend, all the details are there." I was about to ask where the conference would be held when the door suddenly opened and in walked Satan's spawn...Yazmin.

"I'll check the email out on my phone," I said, as I walked out passing Yazmin on the way. She sassed me with her eyes as and just to be a bitch, I put a little sway in my hips and smirked at her before I stepped outside.

Once in my car I took my phone and logged into my work email which was synced to my cell.

I opened the email Jaime sent me and read the itinerary about our travel arrangements.

My jaw almost hit my chest when I read where we'd be going.

"Jamaica," I said out loud inside my quiet car.

Jaime and I would be leaving for Jamaica within the next three days and we would be gone for almost one week; five days to be exact.

I sat and contemplated if I should really be attending another conference with Jaime. The last one I attended we fucked each other's brains out.

But then the more I thought about it, the more it sounded like just what I needed. I needed some time away from everything I was going through. Shit, Jamaica began sounding like exactly what the doctor ordered.

I smiled to myself as I drove out onto the busy street. Then an idea came to me, why should I go on this business trip to such a beautiful island on my own?

An idea popped in my head and I decided to make a detour before I headed home. I was about to take someone along on this trip with me.

I drove in the direction of my sister Sammie's house.

Samantha

$\mathcal{I}$ poured myself my second glass of wine in the last ten minutes. I was slowly turning into an alcoholic!

I paced the living room floor then I walked to the kitchen and paced that floor, then I walked back to the living room so that I could pace some more. I do believe I was slowly losing my mind.

This was all King's fault, that Jamaican asshole. I knew it was totally wrong of me to lay all the blame on him, that I should probably take some responsibility. But who was I kidding? It was a lot more fun to pretend that everything was all his fault.

His cocky ass dropping his towel and practically telling me to get on my knees and suck his nice, long, wide, mushroom-tipped—wait, what was I saying?

"Uughh," I groaned in frustration as I emptied the contents of the wine glass down the back of my throat in one giant gulp. That liquid burned my chest but I didn't mind; that shit felt good as hell.

I'd been like this for the past few days since leaving Kwana's apartment, feeling mortified about the way my visit turned out. I didn't think King would have dismissed me the way that he did and that shit was messing with my mental in the worst way.

The only thing that gave me some satisfaction was that his body still wanted me, even if his mind and heart were fighting it.

As if dealing with King's rejection wasn't enough, my dumb ass husband had been acting really weird lately. His antics were getting worse; he was leaving for work extra early and returning home long after I'd gone to bed.

I had long forgotten the fact that he said we would start a family. I didn't even bother to bring it up again. I decided that I would grow some balls and tell him I wanted a divorce. I was tired of this loveless marriage.

This union only benefitted him and not me. He was in total control of everything, our finances for one, and the fact that I didn't even have my own career was because of him. And what was the thanks that I got for all of this? I'd been cheated on time after time, and I was sick of it.

I knew there was a little more than what I was seeing about what was going on with him. So I decided I would go snooping in his office. With my empty wine glass in hand, I marched over in the direction of his office.

I stopped on the way there to pour myself another glass of pink Moscato. As I poured my drink, I looked up at the mirror over our mini bar and almost shrieked with fright at my appearance.

I looked a hot fucking mess; my hair was a matted nest on top of my head. The shit looked like a beaver might pop out at any given minute. I looked down at my attire and I wore a robe that definitely could use a few spins in my washing machine.

"You need to get it together, Sammie," I spoke out loud as I poured my drink and continued on my way.

Maybe tomorrow I'd get it together. Right now, I needed to be Nosey Nancy and see if my husband was hiding something or if I was just being paranoid.

I pulled open his office door and tip-toed inside. I didn't even know why I tip-toed; nobody was at home but me.

I began rummaging through his desk drawers searching for any type of clue. This shit right here was how I found out Adam was having sex with escorts when I found his credit card statement for the sex shop that he used.

I looked high and low through that office for the next ten minutes, but couldn't find anything. I stood with my hands on my hips as I scanned around the room. The funny thing was, I had no idea what the fuck I was even tryna find.

I was damn sure when I saw it that I would know, however.

My eyes fell on a big winter jacket that hung from a coat rack behind the door. I narrowed my eyes suspiciously at it, finding it strange that he still had it hanging there seeing that it was now summer.

I cautiously walked over to it and found the pockets, shoving my hands inside. My left hand touched what appeared to be an envelope. Grasping it firmly in my hand, I pulled it out slowly and looked down at it.

It was a plain, white, letter sized envelope that had something in it. Biting into my lower lip, I peeked into the already opened envelope and pulled out the contents.

It was a bank statement that had Adam's name to the top.

"This can't be right," I said out loud, as I studied the figures of the opening and closing balance. I looked at the name of the bank and my confusion was only added because I had no idea Adam banked with this particular financial institution. It seemed as though this was a secret bank account.

My mouth almost became unhinged seeing how much money Adam was depositing into this account. Where the hell was he getting these funds from?

I knew damn well his job being a councilman was not this lucrative. The ending balance was over one million dollars; this shit was fucking bananas. *What the fuck was Adam into*?

Realizing that I wanted to know about this money and this secret banking account, I searched the pockets of the coat again but only found a couple of receipts.

Not thinking anything much, I unfolded the receipts and I gasped loudly.

"What the fuck what was he doing shopping in Baby World?" I asked the empty office as I read that the receipt was for a twin stroller. I blinked repeatedly, not sure of what to make of all this.

I opened the other receipt and this one was for baby formula. I looked at the dates on the receipts and they were some months apart.

My heart began thumping loudly in my chest. Did this mean that Adam somehow fathered a baby with someone? And from the looks of it, he fathered twins.

I shut my eyes tightly trying to piece together everything that I held in my hand.

"Oh, here you are," a voice behind me said. I let out a surprised screamed as the contents in my hand went falling to the ground.

I turned around to see my sister, Selah, looking at me as if I were some kind of a mad woman.

"Shit, Selah, you scared the piss outta me," I said, as I bent to pick the stuff up. "I think you should give me that key back," I told her, referring to the key to the house I gave her in case of some sort of emergency.

"I was calling when I came in but clearly you didn't hear me. What you doing in here anyways?" she asked as she came to stand next to me as I finished picking the items off the floor and stood up to face her.

"Nothing, I was just looking for something," I lied, as I tried to stuff the bank statement in the envelope, but Selah snatched it from out my hand.

"Looking for something, more like snooping for something. What the fuck is this?" she asked. Not even waiting for my response, she unfolded the paper.

"You nosey as hell, Selah, give that back." I tried to snatch it from out of her hand but she evaded me.

"Your nigga a millionaire, Sammie. Did you know about this? Can I get a loan?" Selah blurted out questions as she looked at me with one eyebrow raised.

"I most certainly did not know Adam had all that amount of money. I didn't even know he banked there; he hid this from me," I said, as Selah handed me back the bank statement.

"Hid it from you? Girl you hide a bar of chocolate in the cupboard, not over a million dollars in a secret bank account. Adam's ass is trippin'. Sammie, fight him when he gets home. Give his ass the Stone Cold Stunner." Selah's dramatic ass demonstrated the move but I was in no mood for her shenanigans.

"There's something else," I told her, as I handed her the receipts for the baby items.

"Oh, Sammie," Selah said with compassion in her voice. She looked up at me and I felt myself overcome with emotion. "This doesn't have to mean what you're thinking," she said, as she placed her hands on my shoulders and looked me deep in my eyes.

"Twins, Selah, Adam could be the father of twins. Meanwhile, I can't even get this man to touch me after he said we should start a family," I choked up as I spoke from the heart to my sister.

"Sammie, maybe he just assisted one of the women from the community with purchasing stuff for her kids. Think about it, it would be way too risky for Adam to have children running around out of wedlock. That shit would make him look bad." I tried to believe what she was saying…but who was I kidding.

"Selah, we're talking about the man that has sex with escorts for Christ's sake." I rolled my eyes as I walked to place the evidence back in his pockets.

"If it makes you feel any better, Lamar got another bitch pregnant. They having a boy, that's gonna be named after him." I turned to Selah with an astonished look on my face. I didn't know if I should believe her or not.

"Are you tryna be funny right now?" I asked her as I crossed my arms squinting my eyes at her.

"I wish I was. Her name is Shantel Cudjoe and she's been Jaime's patient for the past six months. I found out today that Lamar's her baby daddy when she said his name," Selah said, as she sighed softly looking away from me.

"Oh my god, Selah; I'm so sorry." I rushed to my sister and gave her a big hug.

"It's OK, I'm just glad I already decided to end the relationship." I pulled away from her as we looked at each other and remained silent.

The both of our lives sure were in a mess, that's for sure.

"How's your coochie?" I cracked as I tried to lighten the mood.

Selah laughed at my question.

"My kitty will be fine by the time I land in Jamaica," Selah said, as she did a little dance.

I gave her a curious look, not certain what she meant by her going to Jamaica.

"Jamaica, you're going to Jamaica?" I asked her as she continued doing her silly dance moves.

"Correction, we about to go to Jamaica," she said, as she pointed at the both of us.

"What? Are you on crack?" I asked, as I giggled at her foolishness.

I listened as she explained she was about to go to another conference with her boss in the next three days. And she had this ridiculous idea that I should tag along with her on her business trip.

"Selah, I don't think you gave this much thought. What am I supposed to do when you're at your conference?" I asked, as I looked at her as if she were an idiot.

"Bitch, it's Jamaica. Go sightseeing, go to the beach, drink rum and coconut water all day, fuck a Jamaican nigga...again! Who gives a shit? We both need this break. Come go with me...pleaseeeee," she said, as she used her puppy face as she begged me.

I had never in my life done anything this spontaneous before. I could use the money I had saved for my Yoga studio to pay for my accommodation. And at this point, I couldn't care less about what Adam thought.

"Jamaica?" I asked, as I smiled a little.

"Jamaica, bitch," Selah said, as she began to twerk and we both burst out laughing.

"Rum and coconut water," I began to sing and I joined in twerking along with her.

"Rum and coconut water," Selah repeated as the both of us laughed and twerked like two fools.

Looked like I was about to go to Jamaica!

King

"I should have left your ass at home Kwana," I fussed at my twin sister as we climbed out the taxi in front of Eden Gardens Resort in Kingston Jamaica.

"Shut up big head, I told you that was Kaden that farted, it wasn't me." I cut my eyes at her as I walked to the trunk to retrieve our luggage. Her nasty ass knew she was lying.

"Kwana, you almost killed the driver. That motherfucker eyes started watering and shit." Kwana burst out laughing as if I was trying to be funny. I just shook my head at her as we made our way inside of the hotel.

I admired my surroundings, satisfied with my choice of hotels. This place was nice as fuck; for $800 a night it better be.

"Check-in for the Rocks," I said to the very pretty receptionist behind the check-in counter. When she looked up at me, she began blushing like crazy and I was slightly amused.

"What's good Jo-Anne?" I asked her, reading her name on her name tag. Her eyelash extensions fluttered like crazy as she tried to avoid eye contact with me.

"I'm fine, thank you," she replied shyly, as she searched her computer for my reservation.

I felt Kaden tugging on my arm and turned to him, and he immediately stretched his hands out to me. I smiled at him and took him out of Kwana's hands.

"Come here little man. Meet this pretty lady named Jo-Anne." I continued flirting with her until we were checked in.

With the assistance of the bellhop, we made our way to our room on the second floor.

"This room is so dope," Kwana said, as she wandered around the inside of our spot for the next five days. My phone began ringing in my sweatpants pocket and I put Kaden down so that I could answer it.

Kaden immediately began running around the room to explore.

"Yo, where you at my nigga?" I asked my cousin Mark as I answered his call.

"I'm downstairs at the hotel. You here yet?" I began making my way to the hotel door because a nigga had shit to do.

"I'll be right down," I told him as I ended the call. Kwana emerged from the bathroom and looked at me with curiosity.

"Where you going big head?" she asked, as she walked to me with Kaden hot on her heels.

"Mark's downstairs, we about to head out to the hospital to see Uncle Joseph," I explained to her as I stopped to face her as I walked out the door.

"So what're Kaden and I supposed to do? When would I get to go visit Uncle Joseph?" I rolled my eyes at her because seriously, I should have just left her ass back at home.

"It's a big motherfucking resort Kwana, take your ass down to the pool. You'll visit him tomorrow and we'll go see the rest of our family also," I said, as I walked out the door.

It wasn't hard to make out my cousin, as he stood waiting in the lobby. He wore a Rastafarian colored sweat suit, his dreadlocks hung all the way down his back and he wore a pair of dark sunglasses on his face. He had a thick beard that looked unkempt, which I'm guessing was exactly how he wanted it to look.

"*Rassclat*, look at you my youth. Last time I saw you, you were this tall," Mark said, as he showed me the height with his hand. We gave each other a quick, friendly hug as we greeted one another.

"What's up cousin," I said, as I smiled broadly at him. I got a small hint of weed on his clothing as we hugged.

"Jah has blessed me, I can't complain. Let's go youth." I nodded in agreement as I followed him out of the hotel and we made our way to an all-black BMW. The tint on the vehicle was dark as shit.

"This you Mark? You run things in Jamaica I see," I said, impressed that he was driving the latest series of BMW.

"I man run things, things nah run me, youth," he said, as we both laughed as we hopped in his ride and drove off.

We kept our conversation light, catching up on our family life as he drove us to Kingston Hospital where my uncle was a patient.

My head remained glued to the window as I took in the sights of a place I remembered fondly, even though I left at a young age.

A half hour later, we made our way to my uncle's hospital room. As I entered, I didn't know what to expect but when I laid my eyes on my uncle, he looked as though he had aged significantly since the last time I saw him.

He smiled as I walked into the room, and he seemed genuinely happy to see me; and I smiled back at him.

"Kingsale, I'm so glad you could make it," he said, as I made my way to his bedside, and I immediately bent and hugged him tightly. I was so happy that he survived his heart attack. I was also happy that I decided to visit him.

"I'll leave you two to get some privacy," Mark said, as he turned and walked back out the door, even though he didn't need to leave.

"Pull that chair and sit down for a quick minute," Uncle Joseph said, as he sat upright in his hospital bed. Grabbing the chair in the corner, I pulled it closer to his bedside and sat down.

I looked at my uncle, feeling a bit emotional because I could have lost him just as I did my mother. Uncle Joseph, even though he appeared to look a bit older, looked as though he would make a full recovery. He was hooked up to a heart monitor that beeped softly as it read his heart rate.

"Did Kwana and Kaden come with you?" he asked, and I nodded my head at him. "They gonna come see me before they leave?"

"They are, Uncle Joseph. I promise they'll be here tomorrow," I responded to his question which brought a smile to his face.

"I never thought leaving the U.S. to return to my roots would have given me a heart attack," my uncle said, as he chuckled softly.

"Shit is crazy man, I'm glad you OK, though. I wasn't trying to hear I lost you so soon after losing Mom." I was trying my best to keep my emotions in check. The last thing I wanted was to come all the way to Jamaica to cry like a punk.

"That's kind of the reason I wanted to see you. When I got the heart attack at home I was unconscious for a few minutes before the paramedics came and resuscitated me." I looked at my uncle as he spoke and listened intently, unsure of what he was about to say.

"Your momma ain't happy with you, King," my uncle said, causing me to look at him with curiosity. What the hell was he even talking about?

"What you mean Uncle Joseph?" I asked him, as I knitted my eyebrows together.

"You lost your job, after I did my best to help you get that job. You lost it." The disappointment on his face made me look away from him.

"Man, Uncle, you don't know half of what went down with Mr. Daniel. He lied and said I stole from him. I never stole shit from that nigga," I said, as I felt my heart ice up with the thought of Sammie's stupid husband.

"Tell me this, King, how long have you been fucking that man's wife?" A nigga almost choked on his saliva. I started to cough like a motherfucker and had to beat my own god damn chest.

"What you mean? I ain't never laid hands on that nigga's wife," I said, as I shook my head vigorously knowing damn well the guilt probably showed on my face.

"Kingsale, I am sixty-three years old, you don't think I can't tell when a man and a woman has been having an affair? I suspected something when you were in prison and she kept asking about you." I closed my eyes and pinched them with my index finger and thumb.

These old Jamaican motherfuckers got some type of sixth sense or some shit when it came to these things, I swear.

"But what really sealed it for me was that day when I took you over to their house, your first day on the job. Samantha looked so guilty I just knew there was something going on between you two." I looked over at my uncle and tried to act unbothered by his words.

"I hope she's worth it, Kingsale, because you dumb as fuck for getting yourself mixed up with the councilman's wife." I continued to look at him with a clueless expression on my face, as if I didn't know what he was talking about.

"What was it you were saying about my moms?" I asked him, purposely changing the subject as I gave him a bored look.

My uncle shook his head at me, probably thinking I was one stubborn motherfucker. "When I got my heart attack as I was unconscious, I think I may have been clinically dead for a couple of minutes, your mother came to me," Uncle Joseph said, and I looked at him as if he'd done lost his entire mind.

"What? What you mean she came to you?" I asked my obviously looney toon uncle. I think that heart attack caused him to have mental issues.

"She came to me as I was fighting for my life Kingsale. She's not happy with you, she said you're hurting her. She said she raised you better and she doesn't like what you're becoming." My chest felt tight and I was at a loss for words. I thought maybe my uncle was just fucking with me, but I knew deep down he wouldn't have insisted I came all the way to Jamaica just so he could feed me some bullshit story.

"She told me to give you a message," he said, as he reached for my hand and touched it gently. I locked eyes with him as I waited to hear what he was about to say.

"She said to tell you, don't give up on her. She's about to make you a better man." I swallowed a lump that formed in my throat as I my mouth suddenly went dry.

"Who's she?" I asked, hoping my uncle would be able to shed some light.

Uncle Joseph shrugged his shoulders. "She never said a name, I assumed you would know who she was speaking about." I bit into my lower lip as I looked down at my shoes. The new baby blue Vapormax on my feet tapped nervously as I sat deep in thought.

I wasn't into this bullshit about getting messages from people who were supposed to be dead. But I was curious as to who my mother meant. The only person that came to mind was Sammie. But that couldn't be right; we were barely even on speaking terms.

"OK, thanks for the insight Uncle, appreciate you." I sat there and kicked it with him until visiting hours were over. I told him I'd be back tomorrow to bring along Kwana and Kaden.

"Hey," he said, as I got up to leave. "I know we've never always saw eye to eye. But all I wanted was for you to be a good man, someone that your mother could be proud of. I know you got it in you to walk on the straight and narrow path of life. Fast money isn't always good money. I love you nephew." He reached his hand out to me as he spoke.

I walked back and took his hand in mine and bent to touch the sides of our heads together. "I love you too, Uncle Joseph." The both of us gave a final nod to each other before I turned and walked out the door.

I found Mark outside waiting on me and I walked toward him deep in thought.

"Yo, a *yardie* needs to smoke a fat blunt," I said, as I shoved my hands in my pockets.

"Say no more, let me take you to my side of the ghetto, called Trench Town my youth," Mark said, as he tapped me once on my chest.

Trench Town was definitely a grimey part of Jamaica. An hour after leaving the hospital, I sat in an old wooden house, smoking the biggest blunt I ever saw in my life. The room I sat in was dark, and reggae music played in some other part of the house and I could hear my cousin Mark talking to the other nigga that we met here when we arrived.

"Argh fuck," I groaned, as I looked down at this Jamaican baddie that was sucking the skin off a nigga's dick. Her hair was the color of a peacock's tail and she had glow in the dark nail polish on. Those dick grabbers were glowing a neon green as they wrapped around my shaft.

Don't ask me how I ended up in this position. Mark led me to this room when we got to the house, gave me a blunt that deserved its own page in the Guinness book of world records, and brought a bad ass chick in the room and told her make me feel good.

I knew what my uncle said and all about my mother being disappointed in me. But I promise as soon as I left Jamaica, I would get my shit together, but for right now...

"Aye, open yo' mouth and collect this nut," I instructed her, as I used one hand to jerk my dick off in her open mouth. While the other hand held my blunt to my lips.

Selah

J cursed myself in my head as I felt my phone vibrating in my jacket pocket. I knew it was Sammie calling; she'd been a pain in my ass the past three days since we got here.

I tried to ignore the persistent vibrating as the doctor spoke at the head of the table about new procedures that would soon be introduced when doing ultrasound scans.

I jotted down a few notes as Jaime sat next to me listening attentively. I turned to look at his facial features as he paid close attention to what was being said.

Jesus, this man was so incredibly handsome, I thought to myself as I wet my upper lip with the tip of my tongue. His brown complexion popped in the light green shirt he wore, his waves in his hair rippled like those in the ocean.

His thumb brushed lightly on his thick, pink lower lip as he listened to what was being lectured. My eyes were fixated on his mouth remembering how they felt on my own lips. The way it felt when they touched my breasts and the way it practically covered my entire pussy lips. The one and only time I allowed him to have my body.

Now had I not been so lost in my fantasy, I would have noticed that Jaime's thumb had stopped moving all together. I would have also noticed that he was staring at me staring at him. Our eyes collided and he gave me this look, as if to say, *would you like to feel these lips on your body again.*

I wished that the ground would have opened up and swallowed my ass whole; instead, my phone began vibrating again.

I was never so thankful for Sammie's annoying ass to call me just then. Pulling the phone from out my jacket pocket, I pointed at the vibrating device to Jaime and he nodded his head.

I practically ran out of the room like an Olympic track star, closing the door to the conference room behind me.

"Sammie, I swear to God you annoying as fuck," I said harshly into the phone as I answered her call.

"Really, Selah, I could have been dying and you only just now decided to answer," Sammie said, being her dramatic self she had been for the last three days. I closed my eyes in frustration because she had really been trying me.

"But you're not dying, now are you Sammie?" I said, through gritted teeth.

"But I'm saying suppose I were." I shut my eyes again and counted to ten because I was about to cuss her stupid ass out.

"Girl, what do you want? I have to go back in, the lecture isn't over and I'm supposed to be taking minutes!" I barked at her, as I waited for her to state the purpose of her call.

"I'm bored, Selah, I told you this wasn't a good idea. I have to wait on you to get back from your meetings while I sit and twiddle my thumbs." I sighed softly, understanding her plight.

"Look, why don't you go sightseeing? The lady at the front desk said there is a tour going to Trench Town today. It leaves in the next half hour," I told her, as I looked at the time on the Timex wrist watch I wore.

"Trench Town, what's there about?" she asked, as I began to take slow steps back to the conference door.

"It's where Bob Marley grew up, bitch, don't you know anything?" I scoffed at her in irritation. "Go, have fun; tomorrow will be better. It's the last day of the conference and it ends mid-day, so we can do whatever you wish." She remained silent and I knew that she was contemplating what I said.

"Ugh, fine, I'll go. Hopefully the both of you will be through by the time I get back," she said, and I assured her that I'm pretty sure the conference would be over by then.

"Have fun bitch, and don't call my fucking phone again or I'll kick your ass when I see you," I said, as I laughed before hanging up the phone on her ass just as she was about to say something.

I silently walked back into the conference room and reclaimed my seat next to Jaime.

"Is everything OK?" he asked, as he leaned into me to speak into my ear. His cologne literally fucked my nostrils with its enticing fragrance.

"Mmhmm," I mumbled, as I nodded my head at him, and he gave me a smile in return before turning his attention back to the front of the class.

Just to be safe, I switched my phone off before replacing it inside my jacket pocket. I got comfortable in the over-sized leather chair and listened as I took minutes to the remainder of the lecture.

* * *

EVEN THOUGH *I didn't plan on using my swimsuit, I'm sure glad I packed it with me*, I thought as I laid on my back on one of the lounge chairs out by the pool.

We were staying at the Marriott Hotel in Kingston. At first, when I told Jaime that I invited my sister to tag along on the trip with me, I was unsure of what he would think. He was actually cool with it and didn't have any problems. It's not like he had to pay her way or anything.

Thinking about my sister, maybe I should switch my phone back on just in case she was trying to contact me. I looked to the side of me where I had my phone wrapped in my towel when I noticed someone walking over to where I sat.

I forgot all about my cell phone as Jaime walked toward me in a pair of black basketball shorts and nothing else. I knew Jaime was on some bullshit because his dick swung from left to right as he approached me. *This nigga think he slick*, I thought as my eyes followed him.

Since we got here, we had managed to keep it on a professional level. When we were done with the conference, I would go spend my time with my sister, that way Jaime and I had no reason to be around each other much. We even had our rooms on separate floors.

"I didn't know you would be here, Selah," he said, as he took a seat on the chair next to me. I looked over at him and gave him a sarcastic look because this nigga knew damn well I told him I was thinking about going out to the pool.

"I guess you must not have heard me when I said I was coming down by the pool," I said, as I gave him a look that said he was full of shit.

"I guess I must have missed that," he said, as he gave me his award winning smile, displaying even, white teeth.

I rolled my eyes at him because he was just too damn good looking for his own good.

"Aren't you going in?" he asked, as he tilted his chin toward the pool.

"And risk getting my braids wet, I don't think so," I told him, as I looked out at the water. I felt Jaime's eyes on me as the Jamaican sun beat down on my body exposed in my black bikini.

"You like what you see?" I asked him without turning to look his way, because I could feel his eyes devouring me. "Don't make me tell Yazmin on your ass," I said, as I turned to look his way.

He looked away from me as if he felt guilty by what I said.

"You got jokes," he said, still refusing to look at me.

"What do you see in her anyway?" I asked, as I turned up my nose at him at the thought of Yazmin and her snooty, annoying ways.

"I dunno, what did you see in that nigga who was fucking around behind your back?" A kick to my ribs would have been less painful than his words.

I swear to god I wanted to reach over and smack the shit out of him.

"Maybe you should try minding your business rather than being a judgemental asshole," I spat back at him as he turned and chuckled at the fact that I got upset.

"You started it, Selah, don't be mad now," Jaime said, as he gave me a big broad smile.

"Oh, I now see why you like that bitch. You're a cunt...just like her." His head snapped back at the use of my very derogatory word. Deciding I was in no mood for his childish ways, I grabbed up my towel and got up to return to my room.

I marched as fast as I could in the direction of the elevator. My big booty bounced up and down in my bikini bottom that could barely contain it.

I heard Jaime call out to me but I would be damned if I would give him the time of day. I stood tapping my feet, praying silently that these elevator doors would hurry and open the fuck up before he reached me.

But of course, fate wouldn't let me have this one!

Jaime came and stood next to me glaring at me, his eyes damn near drilling a hole at the side of my head.

Refusing to even look his way, I kept my eyes on the elevator door. As soon as the familiar ding was heard and the doors opened, I ran inside stupidly trying to press the button to my floor before Jaime could enter.

"What the fuck are you doing?" he asked, as he entered the elevator grabbing my hand, stopping me from pressing the button.

Punching his floor number in, which was one floor before mine, the doors of the elevator closed, trapping me in with this maniac.

With my hand still in his, Jaime backed me into the wall as he gave me a death-like stare.

"Have you forgotten that I'm your boss, Selah?" he asked me, as he eased himself against me. We looked into each other's eyes as both of our breathing was short and erratic.

I opened my mouth to reply but not a single word was able to come out.

"What did you just call me? Hmmm." Jaime wrapped his fingers gently around my neck as his gaze fell on my lips. I shook my head, the only movement I could make.

Jaime suddenly dipped his head and bit into my lower lip…hard!

"Ouch," I mumbled softly, as he used the tip of his tongue to soothe the pain of his bite.

The elevator door opened and Jaime pulled away. "I'm about to teach your ass a lesson." Holding me by my upper arm, he all but dragged me out of the elevator to his hotel door.

I fake pretended to try and wrestle out of his grip as he took his key card out his pocket. Holding on to my arm with even more force, he unlocked the door and shoved me inside.

I turned to him as he shut the door behind him and looked at me with rage in his eyes.

I tossed the towel with my cell phone tucked inside of it onto his bed.

Jaime and I challenged each other with a staring match.

"Come here, Selah," he said, as he pushed his hands in his pockets.

I folded my arms under my breasts as I stared at him defiantly as I remained glued to my spot.

"Oh, you think I'm playing with you," Jaime said, as he took a couple of steps to me.

I smiled ever so slightly as he closed the distance between us. Jaime reached up and placed his hand behind my neck grabbing a fistful of my braids, tugging my head back.

"The next time you address me, you address me as boss." I smirked in his face which did not sit well with him. Tugging on my braids even harder, he turned me around and pushed me face first into the wall as he pressed his body into mine.

"You think this is funny?" he asked, as he continued to pull on my hair. I smiled as the pain of his actions burned my scalp. Jaime thought he was doing harm to me? When really, I loved this freaky shit. I lived for it.

"I do think it's funny actually…*Jaime*," I used his name purposely just to annoy him further.

I heard him chuckle from behind me, as his hand reached down to massage my ass roughly through my bikini bottom.

Using his feet, he kicked my legs open further and his fingers inched forward and squeezed my pussy through the fabric.

I moaned loudly as I closed my eyes. I pressed my forehead on the wall in front of me. Jaime's fingers continued to drive me insane as they played with my pussy from the outside of my bikini.

"What's my name?" he asked, as his fingers began shifting the fabric to one side. When the cool touch of his fingertips touched my clit, I moaned loudly again.

"Jaime," I said breathlessly, as I answered his question.

I was given a firm slap on my ass as he removed his hand from my aching bud.

"That's not what I told you to call me, Selah," he said, as he pressed his lips against my ear. Replacing his hand against my mound, this time he made circles in a fast movement, and I suddenly remembered what I was supposed to say.

"Boss, your name is boss," I said, just as he plunged his middle finger deep inside of me.

"Shit," I cursed, loving the feel of how his finger penetrated deep in me.

Jaime untied my bikini bottom, allowing it to fall to the floor as he got on his knees behind me.

"You know how much I missed you, Selah?" he asked as he parted my ass cheeks roughly, exposing my tender flesh for his viewing pleasure.

I hiked my ass in the air knowing I was about to get the best oral sex I'd had in months. My infection was long gone so I was safe to have the sexual encounter I was about to get into.

I took a sharp intake of breath as I felt Jaime's warm, wet mouth wrap around my clit.

"Mmmm," I groaned, as I bit into my thumb, not knowing what to do with myself the way Jaime's mouth was setting my body on fire.

Jaime began flicking his tongue, left to right, then back to front before making circles again, taking pride in his job.

I was panting loudly, not giving a fuck about how I was probably sounding; this shit felt good as fuck. I reached to the back of me and placed my hand to the top of his head, shoving his face into me even more than he already was.

"Get in there," I said, as I rocked my hips against his mouth and he slapped my ass hard, the sound bouncing off the walls of his hotel room.

"You like that?" he asked, as he used his tongue to dive in and out of me, my juices running down my inner leg. My legs began to shake as I fought to keep my balance.

"Yes," I said, as I sunk my teeth into my thumb once again.

"Yes, who?" Jaime asked, as he removed his mouth from me making me whimper with disappointment.

"Yes, boss," I answered breathlessly.

Satisfied, Jaime resumed his assault on my pussy, using his tongue, his lips, his entire mouth to drive me insane.

"Fuck, shit...I'm about to cum," I said, as my entire body shook as I felt my orgasm building.

Hearing me say that, Jaime put my clit between his lips and sucked on that shit, like a baby tugging on the nipple of his bottle. I felt like I was losing my entire mind.

I began moaning loudly as if somebody was murdering my ass as I came hard on Jaime's lips. I was clawing at the wall trying to keep from falling as my knees weakened.

Standing from his kneeled position that he was in, Jaime grabbed a fistful of my braids again. With lips pressed against my ear, he said to me, "Get over there and stand by that desk."

With legs that felt like overcooked spaghetti, I walked to the desk that stood in the corner. I looked back to see Jaime discard his pants, his dick pointing at me as hard as a rock.

He gave me this type of sinister smile and I knew the savage in him was about to come out.

Now standing behind me, he wrapped his hand around my neck.

"You about to pay for your smart ass mouth." Taking hold of my right leg, he hoisted it up to sit at the edge of the desk.

Prompting me to bend my back by pushing me down by neck, I placed my left cheek flat on the desk.

I closed my eyes slowly as I felt his tip at my entrance. With no warning, Jaime plunged deeply inside of me with one stroke, rocking my entire body forward.

"Aahh!" I shrieked out in surprise. The walls of my pussy protested as they ached from the sudden invasion.

Steadying me by placing his hands on either side of my hips, Jaime pumped his length hard inside of me.

I shut my eyes tightly as I moaned with every thrust he delivered. My body jerked forward repeatedly as I gripped the edges of the desk.

"I missed this pussy, Selah. This sweet, juicy pussy," Jaime mumbled under his breath, sounding more as if he was talking to himself rather than to me.

For the next twenty minutes, I remained in that position hollering and begging Jaime not to stop. This shit was hurting like a motherfucker, but I'd be damned if I acted like I couldn't take it.

Once again, Jaime wrapped a handful of my braids around his wrists, his pumps getting faster and even more aggressive.

"Sssss, fuckkkkkkkk!" he hollered out as he came hard, his warm liquid filling my insides.

Collapsing on top of me, the both of us breathing heavily and sweating, I smiled feeling contented.

Jaime slowly exited my body. I promise I had no more feeling in my pussy. I remained in that downward position for a few more seconds before I stood and faced him.

We looked at each other and he smiled at me.

"I really did miss you, a nigga had been going crazy for the last three months," he said, as he admitted to me, his eyes roaming over my body.

I smiled shyly because I had no idea that he missed me just as much as I missed him. He did a pretty awesome job of hiding that shit. I looked down at my feet needing to ask the obvious question.

"So what does this mean for us?" I asked softly, as I waited impatiently for him to reply.

I looked up at him as he walked to me, lifting my chin up to watch him in his eyes.

"It means I don't give a fuck if I'm your boss. I want to be with you." My heart burst into a thousand pieces at his words and I smiled broadly at him.

"You mean that?" I asked, and he nodded his head at me.

I shrieked with excitement and threw myself in his arms. He hugged me tightly as we kissed on one another passionately.

"What about Yazmin?" I asked as I pouted my lips at him, because just saying her name gave me a toothache.

"Let me worry about that," he said, as he pecked me on my nose. "Come take a shower with me," he said, as he took my hand and led me in the direction of the bathroom. "By the way, where's your sister?"

Oh shit! Sammie, I totally forgot all about her.

"Oh, fucking hell," I blurted out as I pulled away from him and raced over to the bed where I had tossed my cell wrapped up in my towel.

Powering on the phone, I muttered a string of curse words as I waited for the phone to come on.

A message popped up on my screen letting me know I had a voicemail. I rolled my eyes knowing full well she was probably cursing me out in this message she left.

I placed the phone to my ear as I listened.

"Selah, what the hell! Did you have something to do with this? Did you set this up?" I creased my forehead as I listened to Sammie because I had no clue what she was talking about.

"What the fuck is King doing here in Jamaica, Selah!"

Samantha

I actually was kind of glad that I came on this tour. It turned out to be very informative.

We were in a place called Culture Yard in Trench Town. The tour guide explained that Culture Yard was the home of a popular community leader called, Vincent "Tata" Ford. Apparently, he was the one that helped Bob Marley out a lot in his younger years when he was starting out to be a musician.

I listened as the tour guide explained each and every instrument and tattered furnishings that inhabited the rooms that she took us to. I shoved my hand in the back pocket of the denim shorts I wore and pulled my phone out.

I attempted to call Selah, to see if her lecture was over, but my asshole sister switched her phone off.

"This is quite interesting don't you think?" a voice said behind me. I turned around stunned and came face to face with a man that looked to be in his late forties.

He was dark in complexion, with a shaved head and a full beard. Average in height with a medium built, he was handsome and his eyes boldly travelled along my body.

Jamaica had a different type of sun I swear, so all I wore was a pair of barely there denim shorts and a plain tank top with a pair of flip-flops on my feet. My short hair was in a low ponytail and I wore no make-up.

"Yes, it is; Bob Marley was a great man," I replied, as I moved a couple steps away from him because he was standing a little too close for me.

"Have you seen Bob's old bus?" I looked at him a little quizzically and he apologized and he held his hand out to me. "I'm sorry, I'm babbling on like a fool and haven't even introduced myself. I'm Marvin Luke," he said as he smiled warmly at me.

"It's nice to meet you Marvin." I returned his smile as we shook hands. "And no, I haven't seen his bus yet, would you care to show me?" Marvin and I stepped away from the other persons that also came on the tour bus with us.

He led me to an old, worn out blue bus in the yard and we stood and admired it together. As I stood there trying to ignore the fact that Marvin was literally undressing me with his eyes.

A small child suddenly ran up to where we were. I had to blink my eyes repeatedly because I swore I was seeing things. This child was the spitting image of Kaden, King's nephew.

He suddenly looked up at me and he smiled with drool running down his chin. I spun around and came face to face with Kwana, she looked at me with a stunned expression as if the feeling wasn't mutual.

"Sammie, what in the fuck, girl what are you doing here?" she asked as she reached forward and hugged me. My arms could barely raise to return the gesture from being taken aback that Kwana was here.

"You're the last person I was expecting to see, Kwana," I said, as we pulled away from each other. I bent and picked up Kaden and kissed his chubby cheeks.

"Did you hear what happened to Uncle Joseph? Is that why you're here?" I gave her a curious look because I was unsure of what she meant.

"Joseph, what happened to him?" I asked, as I handed Kaden over to her.

"Oh, I assumed maybe King would have mentioned something to you, seeing that Uncle Joseph was your driver and all. Uncle Joseph had a heart attack," she said, her words caused me to gasp loudly as I placed trembling fingers to my lips.

"Oh, god. Kwana, is he OK?" I asked, fearing the worst.

"Yeah, he's fine. King and I visited him yesterday and we just got back from visiting him today and we decided to come over here." I was standing there looking at Kwana with eyes as big as grapefruits.

"Ki-King is here?" I asked in disbelief as I pointed my index finger to the ground. This could not be happening right now.

Kwana spun her head around as if she was looking for something…or better yet, someone.

"He's supposed to be around here somewhere," she said, as she searched her surroundings for her twin.

Oh hell no! He was the last person I wanted to see after our last encounter that went so horribly.

"Um, I'll be right back, Kwana," I said, not giving her a chance to respond. I bolted away from her as if my ass was on fire. I found a secluded spot under a tree and pulled my cell phone out my back pocket.

Maybe I was wrong, but I didn't know why I thought Selah had something to do with this. I called her number but her phone was still off, so I decided to leave her a voicemail.

"Selah, what the hell! Did you have something to do with this? Did you set this up?" I all but shouted into the phone. I was breathing heavily as the palms of my hands suddenly began to sweat.

"What the fuck is King doing here in Jamaica, Selah!" I prided myself as a woman who rarely used curse words, but I think under these circumstances it was necessary.

"Hey, is everything alright?" a voice said behind me, almost causing me to drop my phone.

I spun around so fast my neck hurt, only to be faced with Marvin. I had forgotten all about him.

"Yes, I'm fine, I was just surprised to bounce up an old friend of mine," I said, as I pushed the phone back into my pocket.

"Well come on, let's finish our tour. That way I can get to know you better," Marvin said, as he smiled at me and took hold of my elbow in an effort to lead me back inside.

Now tell me why at that very point in time King emerged to see Marvin with his hand on my elbow cheesing at me.

I got deathly quiet as King looked at me and then at Marvin, whose back was to King. So he had no idea of what was about to happen.

King came and stood directly to the back of Marvin and I slowly backed out of the hold he had on my elbow. I guess Marvin saw that I was focusing on someone behind him and he turned around, only to be faced with a pair of angry brown eyes.

"Lehme, holla at you," he said, as he grabbed my upper arm and pulled me away from where a shocked and confused Marvin was left standing alone, probably trying to figure out why I was being taken away from him.

Now standing in a corner of the spacious yard, King continued to glare at me angrily. As mad as he was, my stomach did somersaults at the how fine his ass looked.

He wore simple Nike sweatpants and a plain, V-neck, white T-shirt accompanied with a pair of Timberlands on his feet. His hair looked as if he came fresh out a barber shop and his beard was perfectly trimmed. His chain with the King pendant dangled in front of him.

"You following me? Have you turned into some kind of Norman Bates weirdo?" I snapped my head back so that I could look at King from head to toe because clearly this brother had a whole lot of nerve.

"Excuse you, King, please don't flatter yourself. Now move the hell out my way," I said, as I pushed on his chest trying to get by him because he had already succeeded to get on my damn nerves in such a short space of time.

He grabbed my wrist and held it tight in his hand. His eyes slowly roamed over my body, making me do a little nervous dance on my feet.

"What the fuck are you wearing? Your pants is way too short." My jaw dropped as I stared at him in obvious disbelief.

"Ppffff, last time I checked, my daddy wasn't a Jamaican asshole. Now let go of me and move out my way," I said, as I challenged him with my eyes.

Of course, King was anything but intimidated as he pressed his body against mine. I held my breath as we glared at each other, my breasts smooched on his chest.

"Kwana told you about Uncle Joseph?" he asked, and I was relieved he wasn't trying to start a fight with me. I exhaled softly before I answered him.

"Yes she did, and why didn't call and say something? If you didn't wish to speak with me, at least you could have told Adam." King snorted loudly as he released my wrist and stepped away from me a little.

"I ain't about to tell your dick head husband a god damn thing," he said, as he sucked his teeth.

"How is Joseph doing, Kwana said he's getting better?" I asked, as my eyes admired his body.

"Yeah, he's doing aight. Something you should know though," he said, as he raised his eyebrows at me.

"What's that?"

"He knows about us," King said, and I shook my head because I just knew he had to be lying.

"That's not—you're not being honest," I stuttered a little, knowing damn well King was on some bullshit.

"I promise you, it was like some weird Jamaican voodoo. He said you kept asking about me when I was locked up which was a dead giveaway." I groaned loudly and covered my face with the palms of my hands feeling embarrassed.

"You were missing a nigga, huh?" King said, with a silly smirk on his face.

"No, I wasn't," I replied, knowing I sucked at lying. We got quiet for a few seconds before he started talking again.

"How come you're here, in Jamaica I mean? You here with your *battyboy* husband?" I rolled my eyes at his description of Adam.

"Na, Selah is here on business and she invited me to tag along, she's back at the hotel," I explained, as King listened attentively.

"Yo' husband actually let you leave the country?"

"Not like he really cares." When I told Adam I was leaving for Jamaica all he asked was who was about to pay for the trip. I lied and told him Selah was taking care of everything which made him really happy.

But of course, I paid my own way from the money that I had saved that he knew nothing about. He never even called to find out if I arrived safe or not.

"Where you guys staying at?" King asked, as he lightly brushed his beard with his fingertips.

"Over at the Marriott in Kingston," I answered his question, noticing the way his eyes kept gawking at my body.

"Come on, I'll drop you back over there. We aren't staying too far from where you guys are at." I opened my mouth and began to protest.

"Na, its fine. I came with a tour from our hotel." King gave me a look as if to say why even argue with him.

"Shut up, Sammie," he said, as he took my hand in his and walked us over to find his sister and nephew.

I followed in silence as we found Kwana and Kaden in one of the rooms checking out an antique guitar supposed to have belonged to Bob Marley.

"Let's roll out, Kwana," King said, as he turned to walk back out the door still holding on to my hand.

We walked out into the parking lot, my hand still grasped firmly in King's, to an all-black BMW with a Rastafarian guy seated inside.

"This is my cousin, Mark. Mark, this is Sammie, we about to drop her off at the Marriott," King said, as he opened the back door for me.

"Empress," Mark said with a head nod.

I took a seat in the back with Kwana climbing in beside me with a now sleeping Kaden. King sat in the front with his cousin and we pulled off.

The drive back to my hotel was filled with chatter from King and Mark while reggae music played in the background. Kwana and I caught up a bit, Kaden slept effortlessly in her arms.

"Come on, Sammie," King said, as he turned back to look at me when the car stopped to the front of the hotel. I leaned in and gave Kwana a quick hug and kissed a still sleeping Kaden on his cheeks.

King held the back door open for me as I climbed out. We looked at each other as we walked to the hotel's entrance.

"When do you guys leave?" he asked, as we stopped on reaching the lobby.

"Day after tomorrow," I replied softly, trying not to make any type of eye contact with him. I didn't know how to feel about this accidental encounter as our last interaction was so fucking awful.

"I'mma swing by and carry you and your sister somewhere right quick before you guys leave."

I looked at him a little shocked that he was trying to spend time with me.

"When are you guys going back home?"

"In the next five days; we decided to make it a mini vacation."

I nodded my head, not blaming them for staying at an extended period.

We fell into an uncomfortable silence as I looked around with no real interest at my surroundings.

"Can I see you tomorrow?" King asked me. My face remained calm but on the inside, I was doing a happy dance.

"Ok," I replied meekly.

"Let your sister know what's up. I'll come by and scoop you both up in the evening time, like around 6. I'll meet you right here."

I promise King made me feel like the most unpopular girl in school being asked to accompany the popular jock in high school just then. I smiled at King and nodded my head.

"I'mma hit you up tomorrow," was the final thing he said as he turned and walked out the hotel's entrance.

I practically ran off in the direction of the elevator. Anticipation, excitement and nervousness were emotions I felt wrapped into one.

I made my way to my sister's room and knocked loudly on her door and she opened it up after the first knock.

"Shit, Sammie, are you OK? What in the hell is King doing here, did he see you?" Selah rattled off a bunch of questions as she ushered me inside her room and closed the door behind us.

I walked mechanically over to her bed and sat down and just stared at her. Selah walked over to me with a concerned look on her face.

"Talk to me Sammie. Are you OK?" She caressed my face tenderly as she kept her worried expression on her face.

"I'm fine, I guess I was just really shocked to see him is all," I replied to her, as she took a seat next to me.

"Well damn, tell me everything. Don't leave a bitch in suspense."

There wasn't much to tell so I was done explaining King's and my accidental encounter in a few minutes.

"So you gonna go meet up with him tomorrow?" Selah asked, as she waited on my answer.

"Will you go with me?"

"Bitch, I'm not tryna babysit your ass…no!"

I scoffed at her and gave her a face as I began to protest until she changed her mind.

"Aight fine," she said, finally agreeing to go with me.

"So what did you do while I was gone?" Selah suddenly got this really guilty look on her face, and I narrowed my eyes at her with suspicion.

"Uh-uh, Selah, what did you do?" I asked her as I folded my arms, knowing full well she didn't do what I was thinking.

"I promise, I didn't plan to fuck him Sammie."

I squealed out with excitement as I slapped her arms as I laughed scandalously.

"You are such a hoe, Selah," I told her, as I continued laughing as she eyed me with a serious look on her face.

"I am not, we got into an argument and the next thing I knew his dick was in me."

I laughed even harder at her because she knew damn well she wanted Jaime since the last time she had been with him a few months ago.

"Is your pussy all better? I hope you didn't give that man some funky fish." Selah burst out laughing as she laid back on the bed.

"Fuck you, Sammie, 'bout funky fish. My stuff is all better...shid."

I shook my head as I laid back on the bed along with her.

"He said he doesn't care that he's my boss and he wants to be with me."

I gasped loudly as I turned to look at her. "Are you serious, Selah?" She smiled and nodded her head at me. "I'm happy for you. I think he's a really good guy. Forget about Lamar and move on."

I knew I probably was in no position to be giving anybody advice on relationships, but I wanted to see my sister happy.

"Oh, I'm not about to make amends with Lamar and his dirty dick. But when I do get back, I have something for his ass. I never let him know that I found out about his love child." Selah got this look on her face and I knew my sister, that look meant she was up to no good.

"Selah, what are you about to do?" I asked curiously, narrowing my eyes at her with concern.

"Don't worry about all that. I want you to have a good ass time with King tomorrow and I want you both to get y'all shit together. So when you get back home you can divorce your lying, cheating ass, dog of a husband." I rolled my eyes at her but I agreed anyway.

My stomach had butterflies in them as I thought about the fact that I would be spending time with King tomorrow.

King

I didn't even know why in the fuck I told Sammie I would take her big head ass somewhere. But a nigga couldn't even front. When I saw her standing there with them short-ass pants on with a nigga touching on her, my stupid ass got heated and needed to show my territorial side without even thinking twice about it.

"Where you going?" Kwana asked, as I came out of the shower on my side of the suite I booked. I made sure and booked a suite with our own private rooms so Kwana wouldn't invade my space. But clearly, that wasn't working out in my favor.

"Out, now mind yo' business, big head." My towel was wrapped around my waist as I opened the closet door, wondering what I should wear.

"Shut up, stupid!" Kwana said, as she picked up a pillow and threw it at me. That motherfucker hit me directly on the side of my head.

"The fuck, Kwana, you play too god damn much. Get the fuck out my room before I kick your ass," I said, as I picked the pillow up and threw it back at her.

"Kaden's asleep, so I'm bored," Kwana said, as she laid down on my bed. I'm standing there looking at her as if she done lost her mind. I decided to do something to fuck with her since she didn't want to leave on her own. Unwrapping my towel from on my waist, I tossed it casually on the bed next to her and continued looking for something to wear.

"Ugh, Kingsale, what the fuck is wrong with you!" she screamed as she sprung up from off the bed. She bolted out my room like a Pitbull was hot on her heels.

I chuckled at her and shook my head, happy her nosey ass was out of my hair.

Deciding on an all-black Adidas hoodie sweat suit and a pair of black low-cut Converse, I got dressed, sprayed some cologne on and made my way out of the hotel room.

"Tell Samantha I said hi," Kwana said, as I opened the door to leave. I stopped and looked over at her as she smiled broadly at me as she sipped a bottled water.

"Ain't nobody about to meet, Sammie. Mind yo' business, big head."

I cut my eyes at her before I walked out and made my way downstairs. Mark was about to take me to get Sammie and then I would drop him off so I could have his car for the night.

"Where you about to take your Empress, my youth?" Mark asked, as he drove us over to the Marriott.

"I don't have fucking clue, *rudeboy*."

Mark chuckled and gave me a suggestion just as we drove into the Marriott parking area. I made sure to listen attentively as he directed me on how to get there.

As soon as the car stopped, I hopped out and looked at the time on my cell; it was exactly 6, the time I told Sammie I would be back here.

When I stepped in the lobby I was expecting to see her standing waiting on a nigga, but I didn't see any sign of her. I knew Sammie had a nigga fucked up if she thought she was about to give me the ghost.

I would knock on each motherfucking door until I found her stupid ass. I walked up to the front desk about to find out what room number was hers when I heard my name to the right of me.

I turned and there stood Sammie trying to give a nigga a heart attack with her fine ass.

She wore a red and blue floral print dress that stopped mid-way down her thigh along with strappy sandals. Her hair was all curly and she wore more make-up than she usually did, but not too much so that she looked overdone.

"Hey, I was sitting over there when you walked in," she said, as she pointed to a sofa to the side.

"I didn't see you. Where's your sister?" I asked, only now noticing that she was all alone.

Sammie rolled her eyes before replying, "She claimed to have gotten food poisoning and said she was too sick to come." From the way that Sammie spoke, I figured she didn't believe her sister's story.

"I take it you don't believe that she's sick?" I smiled when Sammie shook her head letting me know her sister was on some bullshit. I for one was happy as fuck that it was just going to be the both of us anyway.

I held my hand out to her and she looked at me, giving me a shy smile before placing her hand in mine. I led her out of the hotel's main entrance to my cousin's car.

"You look really nice," I told her, as we approached the car. She mumbled a soft thank you as I opened the car door for her and she got in.

Thirty minutes after dropping off my cousin at his girlfriend's house, I drove to Maiden Cay Beach. Mark said tonight there was about to be a boat cruise.

I parked the car and Sammie and I hopped out.

"This beach is really beautiful," Sammie said, as her face lit up when she saw the yacht that was being loaded with partygoers.

"Let's go listen to dancehall music and drink until the sun comes up." I winked at her which caused her to blush, and it boosted my ego.

Hand in hand, we made our way to the yacht to party with the other people. I had no idea what I was doing getting myself involved with Sammie again but I knew one thing I couldn't deny, was the fact that I missed her so much.

I knew deep down that I loved this woman, I could give a fuck that she was married. I could give a fuck that I was younger and I sure as hell didn't care that she felt some type of way about our age difference.

All I knew was that I wanted to be around her, I wanted to spend this entire night with her and I wanted to do whatever it took from now until I dropped her back off at her hotel. To prove to Sammie once and for all that she needed to leave her husband, whom she knew nothing about, and be with someone who wanted to spend the rest of his life making her happy.

For the next three hours, Sammie and I drank Jamaican rum punch and danced to songs by Beenie Man, Bounty Killa and of course my nigga Bob Marley.

By the time the yacht was back on shore after the end of the three hours, it was safe to say Sammie had one too many drinks; she was drunk as a motherfucker.

"Oops!" she said way too loud as she tripped for like the tenth time as we walked off the boat.

"Sammie, ain't nobody gon' be catching your drunk ass all night. I told you that shit creeps up on you," I scolded her as I grabbed her upper arm.

Her intoxicated ass began giggling uncontrollably. She stopped walking so she could bend forward and place her hands on her knees as she kee-kee-keed.

Shaking my head at the mess I felt responsible for, I began looking around on the beach as we stood on the sand. I spotted a few beach chairs off in the distance.

Deciding that I needed her to sober up a little before I dropped her off at her hotel because I didn't want her sister to kick my ass, I steered her in the direction of the chairs.

"Where's you *token* me," she slurred as she spoke. And don't ask me what the fuck was token.

"I'm *token* you to have a seat for a minute so you could sober the fuck up. The last thing I need is for you to vomit in my cousin's ride."

She found what I said really funny and she began giggling again. When we got to the beach chairs, I sat down first and pulled Sammie in between my legs to sit.

"Come here drunkie," I cracked, as I wrapped my arms protectively around her stomach. She giggled again as she rested the back of her head on my chest.

We remained in this position for maybe fifteen minutes just looking at the water and saying nothing.

"You good?" I asked her, finding she was too quiet.

"Yeah, I am. Thank you for taking care of me and for bringing me out tonight."

"Don't worry about it," I replied, feeling my body beginning to get aroused from Sammie's closeness.

"King."

"Yeah."

"I'm sorry," she said, and I was unsure of what exactly she was supposed to be apologizing for.

"Why you sorry?" I asked her.

"If I hurt you, when I foolishly went back to my husband. I know now that he doesn't love me anymore and he never planned on us starting a family."

I listened to Sammie and a nigga can't even lie, I felt really bad for her. I knew women dreamed of the picket white fence, with the perfect husband and a house filled with screaming, playing children.

Sammie, however, may never experience that with her fuck boy husband because he was busy fucking someone else and running his own drug block.

"Don't worry about it." What I really wanted to do was let Sammie know everything, that her husband was cheating on her and that he was drug dealer under the alias Big D.

I knew I could never say that though because I wasn't a pussyhole. I would never turn snitch. Sammie just needed to find that shit out on her own.

Sammie suddenly turned on her stomach to face me, catching me off guard.

"I missed you so much, King." We looked at each other with a yearning that I knew we wouldn't be able to fight much longer.

"I missed your stupid ass too," I said, causing her to giggle.

Touching her cheek, I dipped my head so that I could plant a kiss on her lips. I really wanted the kiss to be something sweet but that didn't work out.

Instead, the kiss was raw and almost primitive. We kissed like two people that hadn't been with each other for a minute. Our tongues wrestled with each other's, colliding almost angrily.

I bit her lower and upper lip multiple times causing her to whimper from the pain.

"Are you too drunk for this? Because once I start I'm not about to stop for nothing."

Instead of answering my question, Sammie gave me a devilish stare as she bit into her lower lip. Inching her body down, she shoved her hand down my pants and pulled my erect dick out.

With hooded eyes, I looked down at her as she licked her lips before covering my dick with her warm, wet mouth.

"Argh, fuckkk," I groaned, as I closed my eyes tucking my bottom lip between my teeth. I'm guessing it was a mixture of the alcohol and the fact that she hadn't been with me in a minute, but Sammie was sucking the hell out of my dick.

She shoved that motherfucker all the way down the back of her throat as she moaned while bobbing her head up and down. I liked the fact that I didn't have to tell her how I liked it. She gave me the sloppiest head ever; saliva ran down her chin and her hands as she dealt with her job like an expert.

"Yeah, baby, suck that shit just like that," I said, as I held the sides of her head as I began fucking her mouth.

"Mmmm, mmmm, mmmm," Sammie hummed, as she began making me feel as though I was about to cum. I had to drag her mouth away from me before I had a case of premature ejaculation.

"Take yo' underwear off, and come sit on your King's face." I pushed her off me and she stood up and quickly peeled her panties off.

I slid down a little on the lounge chair and Sammie straddled my body until she was perfectly positioned over my face. With my hands on her ass, I glided her down on my waiting tongue.

"Oh my god," she gasped, as I wrapped my tongue around her pulsing clit. With my hands still on her ass, I rocked the lower half of her body against my wet mouth.

Sammie tasted even sweeter than I remembered. I ran my tongue along her walls, then played with her clit only to bury my tongue deep inside of her.

"King," she moaned my name as she had her hands on the back of the chair balancing her body weight.

Hearing her say my name gave me the motivation that I needed to deal with her *punanny* even more. Using just the tip of my tongue, I flicked it in a quick motion against her clit until it felt like a pebble on my tongue.

Shoving her entire mound in my face, I sucked her hardened nub between my lips. I made sure to hold her in place by keeping my hands firmly on her ass.

"Shit, shit, fuck," Sammie used a string of curse words. I swore the only time she ever really cursed was when I was laying this pipe on her.

Knowing she was about to cum because she began to tremble, I closed my eyes as her orgasm shook her entire being. A burst of warm liquid entered my mouth and I shamelessly drank every drop.

Using a few seconds to steady herself and catch her breath, Sammie raised from off my face. With a satisfied look on my face, I watched on as she hiked her dress up even higher as she turned backwards.

Grabbing hold of my dick, she positioned her body over mine with her back still to me and slid down on my dick.

I closed my eyes briefly at the feel of her familiar warmth and tightness. I enjoyed my view of Sammie's ass bouncing up and down on my lap.

I swear Sammie done turned into a pornstar, the way she was slapping her ass on my thighs and throwing it back like nobody's business. A nigga was tempted to choke her ass and demand to know who taught her all these moves she was doing.

"Grind on it, Sammie," I instructed her as I placed my hands on her hips. Sammie allowed my dick to bury even deeper inside of her and then rotated her hips.

"Oh fuck," I moaned, because I knew I wasn't about to last much longer. Thrusting my hips upward, I pumped inside of her feeling a tightness in my balls and stomach.

Holding her tightly by her hips, I released an animalistic grunt as I emptied my seed inside of her.

"Shit, I missed your ass," I said, as I pulled her down so I could hug her tightly to my chest. I hadn't felt this complete and happy in over three months as I did right now.

Sammie picked up her clutch and took a pack of wet wipes out and began to clean herself off. When she was done, she cleaned me off and tucked my dick neatly back inside of my pants.

"Come here," I told her, and she came and laid on top of me, resting her head on my chest. I held her to me, caressing her back. I never knew that having her in my arms would make me feel this way.

My mind wandered back to what my uncle said and the fact that he dreamt my mother saying don't give up on someone, because that someone was about to make me a better man.

I looked down at Sammie, seeing her eyes fluttering close and then open, as she was fighting not to fall asleep. And at that very moment, I realized I would give everything up for this woman. I would give up the street life, I would give up hustling and making fast money. If it would mean having her by my side on a daily basis.

I would be willing to start a fresh, new life for this woman and it was right there that I knew she was the woman my mother was talking about. Sammie was the woman that was about to make me a changed man... because I had fallen in love with her.

"I love you, Sammie," I confessed to her as I played in her hair. I was greeted with a soft snore. She had fallen asleep, not even aware that I had just confessed my love to her.

Selah

*M*y business trip was now over and I was back at home again. It had been a wonderful five days and I was a little sad that it had to come to an end.

Jamaica was a beautiful island and I couldn't wait to visit there again. Jaime and I were now officially a couple!

I screamed with excitement every time the thought crossed my mind. I had a man whose profession was a gynecologist and not a block boy. My parents were going to be so motherfucking proud of me.

And when they were done being proud of me, they were going to be shocked out of their mind at good girl Samantha. Who done fell for a bad boy. Talk about topsy turvy for your ass.

The night King came and took Sammie on the boat cruise, I faked being sick, because who really was trying to be a third wheel on their date? I knew I, for fuck sake, wasn't. I knew Sammie didn't believe a word of what I said about being sick, but I couldn't be bothered.

Thank God I didn't tag along too. Sammie's hoe ass came back at the crack of dawn with a big ass smile plastered on her face. King had worn that *pum pum* out!

She promised that she was done with Adam and she would be asking him for a divorce so that she could be a free woman to live her life as she pleased. I never felt so proud to say that she was my sister at that very moment.

Of course, I would be waiting to see if she really would be following through on her promise.

I stood in my bedroom and did a twirl as I examined my reflection in the black lace lingerie I wore.

The box braids were bundled up to the top of my head and I even wore a pair of red stiletto heels to complete the look. I had company that was about to come over, company that I was anticipating seeing again.

I smiled at my reflection as I thought about what I was going to do to him when he got here. I bit into my lower lip seductively as I got excited thinking about him.

Satisfied that I looked the part of a sexy temptress, I spun on my heels and made my way to the refrigerator. Opening the stainless steel door, I found the bottle of Moscato wine I bought earlier that day, then I grabbed a pair of wine glasses out of the cupboard.

Walking over to my sofa, I sat down and poured myself a glass of wine as I waited for my guest to arrive.

By the time I was pouring my second glass of wine, there was a knock at the door. I tilted my head to one side and smiled widely as I got up, glass in hand, and made my way over to the door.

I opened that motherfucker and there stood the man of the hour... Lamar Richards.

"Dayummm!" he shouted, as he placed his hand to his mouth as he stared at my attire. I smiled at him sweetly and did a little dance before I spun on the spot so that he could have a good look at what I was working with.

"You like?" I asked, as I was done modelling for him.

"Na, baby, daddy love what you got on," he said, as he clapped his hands together.

"Well come on in then, let's get this party started." I moved out of the way so that he had enough room to get inside the house.

Lamar walked over to the sofa and sat down, barely able to keep his eyes off my curves.

"You want some wine baby?" I asked, as I stood in front of him picking the bottle up from off the center table.

"Hell yeah. I'm so glad you decided to forgive me and give me another chance, Selah. You know I wouldn't cheat on you baby. I honestly don't even know how you got that infection. I told you it had to be from using public toilets."

I listened as he spoke about my STI infection, but I said nothing. Handing him the glass of wine, I sat next to him on the sofa, eyeing him thoughtfully from over the rim of my glass as I sipped my wine.

The remote for the stereo sat between us and I picked it up and hit the power button.

It's gonna burn for me to say this,
But it's coming from my heart,
It's been a long time coming but we done been fell apart

Usher's song "Burn" filled the room and this song was chosen just for this moment too.

Lamar reached out to me and ran his hand up my upper thigh. I playfully slapped his hand away. Placing my wine glass on the center table, I turned to face him. I opened my legs wide so he could get a proper view of my pussy.

"Shit, Selah, you got a nigga on rock; you feel me," he said, as he rubbed his erection through his jeans.

"You missed this pussy, baby?" I asked him, as I rubbed on myself as he practically drooled all over my sofa as he eyed my crotch.

"Fuck yeah, I missed you. Now come here." He snatched for me but like before, I slapped his hand away.

I pulled my lingerie to one side so he could see what he'd been missing as I played with my clit.

"Go upstairs and take a shower," I said, as I continued teasing my clit. "And when you're done, I'm gonna give you everything you deserve, everything you could ever dream of." I smiled naughtily at him.

I didn't have to say anything else. Lamar sprung up from off that sofa and headed upstairs. I followed him and stifled a laugh as his hurried steps caused him to trip twice.

"Gimme your clothes baby," I instructed him as he stood in the middle of my bathroom floor and stripped out of his Levi jeans, his plain, black T-shirt and a pair of Huarache sneakers.

When he handed his clothes to my outstretched hand, I folded them neatly as he hopped in the shower.

"I'll be back, let me go put these on my bed for you."

"Ok baby, I'm about to take this shower right quick," Lamar said as I walked out the room.

Once out of his eyesight, I kicked off my stiletto heels and I raced downstairs and threw his clothes and sneakers in the trash. Making my way back to my bedroom in record time, I picked up the brand new leather belt that laid on top of the bed.

I walked over to my dresser and picked up the bottle of baby oil. Lamar was about to thank Regina King and the movie *This Christmas* for what was about to happen to his ass.

I walked back to my bedroom and Lamar was still having his shower. Emptying the contents of the baby oil in front of the shower where he would step, I held the leather belt in my hand as I called out to him.

"Oh, by the way, Lamar."

"Yeah, baby."

"How's Shantel and your unborn son doing?" I asked. I knew I must have stunned his ass because he grew very, very quiet.

"H-huh? What's that you said baby?" his stupid, lying ass asked as he stuttered.

"Bring your ass out here and let me holla at you right quick." I stood a safe distance away from the baby oil on the floor as I swung around the leather belt in my hand casually.

Lamar peeked his head out from the shower and the moment he saw my stance and the expression I wore on my face, he already knew I was on some bullshit.

"Really, Selah? This why you called a nigga over here? I thought I was about to get some pussy." My face contorted at his statement...the audacity!

"You thought you was about to get some what nigga! Some pussy, after you had my pussy sneezing for a whole week. A bitch had to go on some antibiotics behind your dirty dick ass!" I yelled at him as I continued to swing the belt around.

"I swear you bugging now. I never gave yo' ass a god damn thing!" Lamar actually was yelling at me right now. I'd had enough of this shit.

"Lamar, bring your stupid ass out that shower so I could beat yo' ass again," I threatened him with a tight jaw as I mean mugged him.

Sucking his teeth as loud as he could, he turned the faucet off and pulled the shower curtain to hop out. I was ready as ever as he placed his feet on the floor and walked out.

OK, so you know like in the movie when dude stepped out he simply slipped and fell, then Regina began beating the shit out of him with the belt.

Well that shit clearly was really a movie! See what had happened was, when Lamar stepped out one foot at a time, this nigga done slipped and fell back, hitting his head…and knocked out cold!

So now I'm standing there afraid to step foot in the baby oil, looking down at an unconscious Lamar not knowing what to do.

A bitch started to straight panic.

"Lamar, Lamar," I called out to him, beginning to get worried that I just committed a murder. I started to have an anxiety attack so I decided to do the only thing that would make sense.

I beat his ass anyway. I might as well try to bring his unconscious self awake.

"Lamar, get the hell up."

Whack!

I hit the belt over his bare ass, and it instantly turned red because I hit him with some force.

"Lamar!" I shouted at him again.

Whack!

This time I hit the belt across his back. I guess he thought he was probably back in the slavery days because that shit sure woke his ass up.

"Aahh! The fuck!" he yelled out as he tried to stand up, the blow to his back shocking him.

Lamar looked like a newborn calf trying to take his first steps as he tried unsuccessfully to stand on his feet.

Not wasting any time, I fired another lash his way, cracking the belt on his arms.

"Arghh! Selah, I swear I'm gonna kill you when I get up from off this floor," he said, before falling flat on his face again.

"Fuck you, Lamar! You had a bitch fucked up," I screamed down at him as I launched another strap against his flesh. His skin now turned a lovely bright red color.

"You gave me an STI—*whack*—then your loud mouth baby momma

boasting that she's naming her baby after the father Lamar Richards —*whack*. After all this time you had been cheating on me Lamar! *Whack.* No wonder your ass was always broke."

My chest shook with all the rage that I kept bottled up inside of me for the past weeks. I kept hitting him in between my talking to him.

"OK, OK, I'm sorry aight. I didn't know what to do when I found out she was pregnant. I didn't even want the baby. I swear to you," he pleaded with me as he laid on his back looking up at me.

"That shit hurt Lamar, like it hurt for real. How could you do me like that?" I felt myself getting emotional even though I swore that I wouldn't.

"Selah, I'm sorry. I promise I'll spend the rest of my life making this up to you. If you would just forgive me. I love you too much to let you go." Lamar got such a sympathetic look on his face, and I was almost tempted to believe him…almost!

Remembering seeing the image of his baby while Shantel did her sonogram, I felt angry all over again and raised my belt slowly. Making sure to keep eye contact with Lamar so he would see this one coming.

"Don't you hit me with that motherfucking belt again, Selah." I paused and raised an eyebrow at him, wondering what he was about to do about it.

"What you say? Don't what?" This time I turned the belt so the buckle of the belt would connect to his skin instead.

Whack!

"Aahhhhh, ouch, you fucking, crazy, bitch!" Lamar roared at me as spit flew out of his mouth as he fought to climb to his feet again.

This time he gripped the walls and somehow was able to steady himself.

Oh shit! I screamed in my head, this nigga was about to get up. This shit definitely didn't happen in the movie either.

With eyes as big as ping pong balls, I suddenly bolted out of the bathroom for the bedroom.

"Why you running, Selah!" Lamar shouted behind me. I ran to the top drawer of my dresser and tapped my hand around to the back of the drawer just as I heard Lamar enter the bedroom.

"You think you crazy, Selah? I'm about to show your ass who's really crazy."

My heart was beating like a fucking Cherokee drum in my chest.

Where the fuck was it? I began to panic, wondering if I had somehow removed it and couldn't remember.

Just as my fingers brushed against the smooth steel, I felt Lamar's hand grab my shoulder.

Holding on to the handle of the gun, I pulled it out just as Lamar roughly spun me around.

In one fluid movement, I pointed the gun directly to the middle of his forehead.

His eyes grew wide with fear as he stared at me as if he was wondering if I had the guts to pull the trigger.

"Now what you about to do, is turn your naked ass around. Walk out my door, jump your naked butt in your car and go to your pregnant baby momma," I told him calmly as I challenged him with my cold, angry eyes.

"You a crazy bitch," Lamar said, as he clenched his jaw in anger.

"And you ain't nothing but a dirty dick nigga that never deserved my love. Now get the fuck out my house before I shoot your ass."

Giving me one last icy stare, Lamar turned and walked out my door and out of my life…for good!

Adam Daniel

"*A*re you sure you want to do this?"

I turned to Officer Alexander who was beginning to sound like a big pussy right about now. We sat next to each other in an unmarked police vehicle.

"Yes, this is what I want to do. What, you scared nigga? 'Cause I don't need no pussy niggas on my team." He looked over at me and scowled, clearly not approving of the description I used for him.

"Man, shut the fuck up. I've been down with you from ever since and now you wanna call me a pussy. You better have some fucking respect for me." We exchanged disapproving glances with each other until I looked away.

"Fuck all that. But this is definitely what I'm gonna do. That nigga had the nerve to show up at my office and threaten me in my place of business. Na, fuck that lil' young nigga. I want him fucking dead."

I looked out the window and over at the corner from where we were parked. A bunch of young hustlers stood out on the block and every couple minutes, someone approached them to buy their shit.

I grinded my teeth in anger because King and his block boys were making a lot of money. In the meantime, my crew was barely making the amount they should have been making at the end of each week.

That shit was beginning to depress the fuck out of me. Then King had the nerve to show up at my office talking out the side of his neck to me.

"Is he back from Jamaica yet?" Officer Alexander asked me.

"Yeah, he came back a week ago. He went to visit his uncle who used to work for me. Apparently he had a heart attack." I had gotten a call a few days back that Joseph had a heart attack, so I wired a couple hundreds to his account in Jamaica. I didn't really have any beef with Joseph; his nephew, on the other hand, was a motherfucking problem.

"So how do you plan on taking him out?" I smiled at his question because I had put a lot of thought in this.

"When he's making his rounds collecting his money at the end of the month. I'll follow him and take his ass out." I wasn't a cold blooded killer or nothing, but I for damn sure wasn't about to hesitate putting a bullet between King's eyes. I was sick of that nigga.

"You plan on doing that shit by yourself?" Officer Alexander asked me.

I looked over at him and nodded my head. "Hell yeah, you don't know just how much I want to kill that fool. He's too damn cocky for my liking." I looked on as King's boys had a rapid flow of customers and a scowl formed on my face.

"Let's go man, I can't stand them lil' niggas profiting more than they should. Drop me back off at my girl's place," I instructed him, and he didn't hesitate to start up his car.

The drive back over to Sandy's house was silent. I was deep in thought about how I planned on executing King. Whatever I did, I had to make sure nothing came back to haunt me. I had to be as careful as possible and not get caught.

We pulled up at Sandy's and I opened up the door getting ready to hop out.

"When you ready to put him to sleep, let me know so I can be the first officer on the scene and I got you. I'll take it from there and be sure your tracks are covered," Officer Alexander said, and I smiled over my shoulder at him. I guess he wasn't a pussy after all.

"I don't know why you over there smiling, that shit is going to cost you a mint my nigga. Hop your ass out my shit." Shaking my head at this dirty ass cop, I got out his car and he sped off.

I looked toward the front door of Sandy's house and it suddenly opened. My car was parked in her driveway, just where I left it before I left with Officer Alexander.

Sandy stood at the entrance of the doorway and looked my way as I walked to her. All I knew was she better not start no shit, because I wasn't in the mood.

She moved to one side with an odd expression on her face as I walked in through the door.

"Why you looking like you constipated, what's wrong with you?" I asked her as I walked over to where my twins were in the playpen in the middle of the living room.

Alexandria was awake, sitting down as she gnawed on her teething ring. Alex was fast asleep next to her. I swear he was always asleep, Alexandria was a lot more active than him.

Reaching into the playpen, I scooped her up in my arms and she started to giggle.

"How's Daddy's little princess doing," I cooed at her, as she grabbed my lips with her chubby fingers.

Sandy came to stand in front of me with the same irritated look on her face. I was trying really hard to ignore her because I just knew she was about to get on my last nerve.

"I can't do this anymore, I think we should break up." I rolled my eyes at her and sighed heavily because I was right, she wanted to start some shit.

"I'm not in the mood for your crazy antics, so miss me with all that noise," I told her as I focused on raining kisses on Alexandria's cheeks, who was beginning to fall asleep.

"You think I'm playing, Adam? I ain't doing this anymore. I was stupid in the first place to think you would leave your wife for me. All you're doing is stringing me along, you will never leave her to come be with us." I looked away from Alexandria who was now fast asleep and focused on her stupid ass momma.

First thing was, Sandy was 100% correct. I would never leave Samantha for her. I must admit, I did care about Sandy and I loved the fuck out of my kids. But let's be real here, I couldn't divorce my wife and run off with an escort!

That shit would be preposterous. I didn't see why Sandy couldn't just be satisfied with all that I provided for her and play her part as a good and loyal side chick.

"Maybe you should go take a nap or something and stop talking crazy, Sandy," I told her, as I stood up with a sleeping Alexandria and placed her in the playpen next to her brother.

"I've made up my mind, Adam. I'm about to take my kids and leave town or something." Now you see, this was where Sandy was about to get my full attention.

Walking away from my kids, I kept my eyes on Sandy as I took slow, cautious steps toward her.

"What you just say to me? You about to take my what?" I said softly, as I was now standing directly in front of her.

"I said I'm sick of this and I'm leaving and taking my ki—" Not giving her a chance to complete her sentence, I lifted my hand and in one quick movement I wrapped it against her neck.

Sandy clawed at my hands with wide, terrified eyes as she sputtered out of breath. Her eyes began watering and she looked like she was about to pass the fuck out.

I released her abruptly and she fell to a heap on the floor at my feet.

"Don't you ever, in your motherfucking life, threaten to take my kids away from me again," I scolded her as I pointed my index finger at her. "You only think about doing some reckless shit like that and I wouldn't hesitate to dead your stupid ass."

Seeing that she done pissed me all the way off, I decided it was best I took my ass on home.

I crossed over her and made my way to the front door.

"Adam, please wait, don't go...I'm sorry," Sandy said, as she pleaded with me.

I didn't even bother turning around to give her another look. I walked out the house and slammed her door shut.

Samantha

Once again, I was back to cheating on my husband. But I couldn't care less that I was!

It had been almost a month since I was back from Jamaica with Selah, and I was so glad that I allowed her to talk me into going. If it wasn't for her, I would not have been able to rekindle my romance with King.

Like before, King and I were using every free moment to be with each other. It was actually easier than the previous time because my husband was so engrossed in whatever he had going on he didn't even know that I wasn't at home as often as I should be.

Besides, I had finally made up my mind that I was about to tell him rather than ask him for a divorce. It was obvious our marriage was just a big sham, and it didn't make a bit of sense.

I wasn't happy and it was no secret Adam wasn't about to be done cheating on me, so we might as well pull the curtains down.

"So did he notice yet that most of your things are gone?" King asked me as he rubbed the heel of my foot as we sat on his bed.

"Nope," I replied, as I stuffed my mouth with a handful of flaming hot Cheetos. King was referring to the fact that I had been secretly bringing my belongings over to his place which was where I would be staying once I told Adam I was leaving him.

"See, I told you he was a *battyboy*. How would he not notice his wife was moving out slowly but surely from his own home?" King shook his head in disbelief. "I think you should just leave from now. Why wait until the beginning of next month to let him know you want to divorce him?"

"There's some stuff I want to wrap up over at the house. I'm pretty sure I'll be done by the end of this month or the beginning of next month at the latest."

"Good, I can't wait to have you all to myself," King said as his hand began to travel higher under the dress I was wearing.

"Damn, Sammie, would you stop eating that shit? That's like your third pack of Cheetos."

I stuffed more of the cheesy puffs inside my mouth, unable to get enough of the snack.

"I swear this shit tastes so good," I muffled out in between chews.

King shook his head at me and snatched the pack from out of my hand and tossed it on the floor.

"Really, King? I wasn't done eating that," I fussed as he lifted me up and brought me down to straddle his lap.

"How 'bout you give me just as much attention as you've been giving that bag of Cheetos." He wrapped his hand around my waist and licked his lips lustfully.

"Oh, you want some attention," I said, as I slowly dipped my head, bringing our lips closer.

"Yeah, give your King some of that good, good," he said, as he thrust his hips upward playfully into my already moist center.

I giggled as I kissed his lips, pushing my tongue into his mouth.

"You still think our slight age difference is going to be a problem for you once you move in with me?" King asked, as he pulled his lips away from mine.

I couldn't even lie, at first King being three years younger than me bothered me somewhat. But King and I had such a strong connection and beautiful vibe, I was able to brush my being older than him to the side.

"No, I kind of like it now." He raised an eyebrow suggestively at me.

"You kind of like it now, why?" he asked me, as he began caressing my thighs.

"Well, younger men got that stamina going on in between the sheets," I said, as I giggled at the way he looked at me.

"Oh, your lil' nasty ass likes that." King's hand began inching closer to my pulsing pussy that was moist as hell, and he hadn't even begun to have his way with me yet.

"Yeah, I do," I said as I bit my lower lip as King used his index finger to trace the outline of my pussy lips slowly.

"Shit, King," I moaned, as he rubbed my clit through my underwear.

I closed my eyes as the lower part of my body gyrated against King's fingers. As I straddled his lap, I opened my legs even farther apart, making sure to give him proper access to use my body to his liking.

"Open your eyes, Sammie, and look at your King."

My eyes fluttered open slowly and focused on him. His eyes were low and his light brown pupils were now dark with desire.

"I want you to look at me because I'm about to make you cum real hard." Just those words alone made me moan even louder.

"Reach down and shift your panties to one side for me," King instructed me. With shaky fingers, I did what I was told and moved my underwear to one side. Our eyes never looked away from each other's.

"Skin up this tight *pum pum* for me." Whenever King said that to me, he always made me blush because those words were so raw and dirty.

King made me do a lot of dirty things with him already, so this time was no different. Reaching in between us, I used one hand to spread my pussy lips apart for him.

King looked down and tilted his head to one side as his eyes raped my sex. With his index and middle finger, he inserted them into my dripping slit, moving them slowly inside of me.

"Ssssss," I hissed, loving the way he felt, enjoying how easy it was for him to bring my body to life.

"You like that?" he asked, as he used his fingers from his other hand to circle my clit.

I dropped my head back and closed my eyes again. I couldn't form the words because the way King's fingers were working my insides, I knew I would be cumming and hollering out his name in a couple minutes.

"Na, look at me, Sammie," King said, as his fingers came to a stop.

I whimpered at him as I lifted my head and gave him an irritated glare.

"Keep looking at me." His fingers started up again, in a nice, slow pace as they dived in and out of me.

I wanted so many times to close my eyes because to me, when I closed my eyes it was as if I enjoyed the pleasure that his fingers gave me even more.

But I knew King wanted me to keep them open, so I did.

"Fuck, right there, baby," I said, as King kept stroking my G spot. I could hardly contain myself as I humped his hand as we looked at each other.

King's finger strokes quickened and I knew I wasn't going to last much longer. Biting into the corner of his bottom lip, King got this devious look on his face as the walls of my pussy gripped his fingers.

"Yeah, Sammie, cum for me." Placing my hand on top of his that toyed between my thighs, my mouth opened and formed a silent O as my pussy creamed all over his fingers as my orgasm slowly but powerfully took over my body.

"Fuck, yeah, baby," King said, as I spasmed from my orgasm on his hand. My breathing was loud and coming out in short gasps as I struggled to calm down. King was right when he said he was about to make me cum harder.

Leaning into me, King kissed my mouth roughly, shoving his tongue forcefully inside. I wrapped my hand around his neck as I deepened the kiss.

Tearing his lips away from mine, he placed his mouth against my ear.

"Take yo' clothes off, and *mek me deal with this punanny*."

Half an hour later, with a sore body and an even more sore pussy, King and I laid in bed as I munched on the Cheetos he took from me earlier.

"Really, Sammie, you about to get crumbs in a nigga's bed." He sucked his teeth at me as I stuffed my face. "Why you even eat that? Shit can't be good for your health."

"I swear I've been eating this all week. Have one, it's so good," I told him, as I held up a cheesy curl to his lips. He shook his head, letting me know he didn't want it.

But I insisted anyway and kept prying it onto his lips. He finally opened his mouth and I popped it in.

"Ew, that shit is nasty as fuck," King said, as he coughed uncontrollably. I swear he was about to bring a lung up.

"You don't know what you're talking about," I said to him.

King mumbled that I was crazy for enjoying that garbage and switched his position, resting his head on my lap as I continued eating.

"You know, back when we were in Jamaica, the night I took you on that boat cruise, you got drunk as shit off that Jamaican rum." I laughed at his words because I didn't think I would have gotten as drunk as I did. That rum punch tasted like juice.

"I said something to you that night, but your drunk ass had already fallen asleep and you didn't even hear a word I said." I paused mid-way from placing a cheese curl in my mouth. I had no idea what he was talking about.

All I remembered about that night was we had some amazing make-up sex and we slept on the beach that night in his cousin's car.

"What did you say?" I asked him, as he looked up at me. He studied me for a few seconds and just like that, he changed the subject of our conversation.

"Did I ever tell you why my uncle called me over to Jamaica in the first place?" I pulled my eyebrows together, confused as to why he just switched the conversation up like that.

I shrugged it off and answered his question instead. "No, you didn't. Why did he tell you to come home? I assumed it was because he had a heart attack."

King's uncle had made a full recovery. I had even gone to visit him before I left Jamaica. King took me to see him, and I remembered Joseph didn't even look at all surprised to see me, which was odd.

"Na, that wasn't the only reason. He told me my mother came to him when he had the heart attack and was unconscious, and told him she wasn't happy with me and how I was living my life." I looked away from him because over the past couple of weeks, we spoke about his lifestyle.

I told him I didn't particularly like his choice of profession but I wasn't about to tell him what to do either.

"Then he said something kind of strange." I looked back down at King as I waited for him to give the remainder of his story. "He said my mother wanted him to give me a message."

"A message, what message?" I asked, as I got really intrigued by this conversation. I'd heard people say that they dreamt of a deceased relative before and were given warnings.

"She told him to tell me, 'don't give up on her, she's about to make you a better man.'" My eyes grew wide for a quick minute at what King had revealed.

"She! Who's she?" I queried as I looked at King, wondering if I should get ready to hit him upside his head. Thinking he had another woman or something.

"Relax, I see you getting that crazy look in your eyes and shit. I believe she meant you." He pointed his index finger at me and I smiled.

"Since we got back together, I've been doing some thinking and I think I could chill out on selling drugs. I mean, a nigga got mad money saved up, not like I'm about to starve or nothing."

The smile on my lips grew wider because I couldn't believe what I was hearing. King was finally contemplating leaving his life of making fast money behind.

"I also think it's time for you to go on ahead and open up your studio." The smile faded from my face because I had used some of the money for my trip to Jamaica.

"I can't even focus on that right now. I used some of my savings," I confessed to him, as I got a sad look on my face.

"Don't even worry 'bout all that." King suddenly got up from off the bed and walked over to his walk-in closet. I looked on in curiosity as he came back with a stash of money in his hand wrapped with rubber bands.

Sitting on the bed again, he placed five rubber band stacks on my lap. My jaw was on my chest as I looked at all that money right at my fingertips.

"What's all this?" I asked him as I picked up each stack and examined it. Trying to make a mental count of how much money sat on my lap.

"That's over $50,000. I think you should get a bigger place than the one you were looking at a few months ago."

I shrieked with excitement as I threw myself at him, hugging him tightly because I swear I didn't deserve this man. I couldn't wait to finally open my very own Yoga studio. I was so passionate about it.

"I'll call up my real estate agent and see if she could squeeze me in this Saturday to look at some places. Would you come with me?" I asked him, wanting him to be a part of the decision I made.

"I have to collect my money from my block boys on Saturday. I guess you could tag along with me and when I'm done, we could go handle your thing." I shrieked again and hugged my man who showed me in a few months how it really felt for a man to appreciate his woman.

King moved the money from off my lap so that he could place his head back on my thighs. I looked down at him again and played with his hair.

"What did you say?" I asked him after a couple seconds passed, causing him to look at me confused.

"What you mean?"

"Earlier, you said back in Jamaica you said something to me but I didn't hear you. What did you say?" I asked him.

King reached up and placed his hand on my cheek, a sincere look in his eyes.

"I told you that I loved you." The world came to a stop right at that very moment. Everything, and I do mean everything, stopped moving as I looked at King. Did I hear him correctly?

"Yo-you said wh-what?" I stammered out, wanting nothing more than for him to repeat what he said.

"I love you, Sammie. I think I fell in love with you the first time I saw you, if you believe in that sort of thing." King had me stuck on stupid because I knew for a fact that I felt exactly the same way.

"Well damn, you just gon' stare at a nigga and not say nothing?"

"I love you too, King," I replied, as we both smiled at each other.

"Ah shit, bring yo' Cheetos mouth here girl," King cracked as I giggled.

I bent my head and we kissed as we sealed our love for each other.

Within the next few weeks, I would be a divorced woman and King and I would finally be able to live out the rest of our lives together...or so I thought!

Selah

*J*aime's last patient for the day was gone so I finally got the chance to be alone.

I stood in the bathroom with the rectangular box in my hand, wondering if I should even be worried.

I hadn't gotten my period last week and the thought occurred to me that I may be pregnant. I took one of the pregnancy tests that we kept at the office and came in the bathroom to take it.

But now that I was here, I was scared as hell to even open up the box.

"Maybe I'm tripping for no reason," I spoke to absolutely no one as I tapped the box in the palm of my hand. My mind went back to the trip in Jamaica and I knew if I was indeed pregnant, that's when it happened.

I groaned softly at the memory and shook my head for being so careless. I decided to bite the bullet and just go on ahead and take the test. I was pretty sure maybe I was a little stressed and that was the reason behind my being late.

Taking the white stick, I unbuttoned my pants and pulled down my underwear and peed on the stick. Placing the white wand down on the toilet tank, I cleaned up myself and adjusted my clothes.

I turned my back to the test as I waited for the time to pass so that I could check on the results.

I thought to myself, *what the hell I was about to do if that test was indeed positive.* It was definitely way too soon for Jaime and I to become parents. We never even spoke about having kids. I didn't even know if he wanted to have any.

Jesus Christ, what did I get myself into? If I was indeed pregnant, Jaime would probably dump my ass and then I would become another statistic of a single black mother.

A part of me wanted to be a mother so bad. Seeing all these women come through this office with their pregnant stomachs, with hearts in their eyes as they saw their babies on the ultrasound machine, I wanted that also. I wanted to experience carrying and birthing a child just like any other female.

Exhaling loudly, I spun around with my eyes closed. I picked up the test and slowly peeked at the results.

The expression on my face stayed the same as I looked at test in my hand. I blinked a few times as I continued to stare at the white stick.

The white stick that was about to change my life for the next nine months…I was about to have a baby.

Water pooled in my eyes at the thought that a little human was now growing inside of me.

I began giggling hysterically as I just stared at the test in my hand. This felt surreal as fuck…I was pregnant!

Do I tell Jaime now? Do I wait until I know how he really feels about having kids?

I bit the inside of my cheek as I thought about what I should do. It really wasn't fair that I kept this news all to myself. Jaime should know that he knocked my ass up.

I took some deep breaths and decided that I would go to his office with the test in hand and let him know we were about to be parents.

I shoved the pregnancy test in my jacket pocket and proceeded to exit the bathroom. As I opened the door, voices could be heard and the voices sounded as though they were angry.

My steps slowed down a bit as I tried to place whose female voice I was hearing. I knew the male voice was Jaime's but I wasn't sure who he was talking to…until I got closer.

"Really, Jaime, so that's it, you not about to try to give us another try," the female voice said, and I knew that it was none other than Yazmin.

Jaime told me that he broke it off with her when we got back from

Jamaica. According to him, they never really clicked and he was just entertaining her as a way of keeping his mind off me.

He said they only had sex a handful of times and it wasn't even all that great. So can somebody please tell me why she was here right now acting all desperate and shit?

I walked to the front area of the office and as always, she was dressed in her designer attire, looking like a million dollars.

Jaime was standing with his arms folded, an exasperated expression on his face, as Yazmin glared daggers his way.

Not even trying to get in between their argument, I decided that I would just leave and meet up with Jaime after at his place.

I quietly made my way to my desk and gathered up my belongings. I knew their eyes were on me without having to look their way.

My keys in hand, handbag over my shoulder, I looked at Jaime and smiled. "I guess I'll talk to you later," I said softly, as I attempted to make my way out.

"I'll swing by your place when I'm done here," Jaime said, as he returned my smile.

As I walked past Yazmin, she suddenly shoved her body in front of me so that I had to come to a stop.

I looked at her, not in the least bit intimidated in any way.

"I know I did not just hear you correctly Jaime," she said, as she looked at me then looked over my shoulder at Jaime. "Why are you about to swing by her place? Are you two seeing each other behind my back?" her delusional ass said, as she cut her eyes at me.

Not even about to entertain this clown, I looked over my shoulder at Jaime. "You better get your girl before I do," I said, and gave him a look that said I wasn't playing.

I tried to get by Yazmin and once again, she blocked my path with her body.

"Yazmin!" Jaime shouted behind me. But I was already about to put my hands on her. I placed my belongings back on my desk, ready to square up to fight her ass.

"What you about to do project Barbie?" Yazmin said, as she tugged on her earrings as she took them off.

"Come over here and let me show you," I said, as I lunged for her. The only thing I was able to grab was the collar of her shirt because Jaime held me by waist and pulled me back.

"Chill out, Selah," Jaime said, as he got between Yazmin and I.

"You're screwing your assistant Jaime, really?" Yazmin eyed me with disgust as Jaime put me to stand behind him as if I were a badly behaved child.

"I told you weeks ago it was over, Yazmin. Why the fuck did you even bother to come over here?"

"Because I thought we could somehow work out whatever the problem between us was, Jaime," Yazmin said, as she placed her earrings back in her ear.

"There's nothing to work out. We didn't have shit in common and all you did was talk about yourself." I snickered behind Jaime just to annoy her even more.

"Clearly, you prefer ghetto bitches with infected va-jay-jays," she said, as she sneered her upper lip at me.

My blood boiled with rage as I lunged at her once again for talking about my STI.

Jaime was able to grab me once again before I even got a hold of her this time.

"Kiss my ass bitch," I spat at her, which only made her made her smile.

Turning her sights back to Jaime, she gave him a look of disgust. "I should have known I was too much of a classy woman for you."

"Yeah, that's it. Can you leave please? I'd like to lock up." Rolling her eyes and sucking her teeth loudly, Yazmin spun in her designer heels and walked out the door. Making sure that she slammed it on her way out.

Pushing Jaime out of my way, I retrieved my stuff from the desk as I was about to leave, not bothering to say a thing to him.

Jaime grabbed my wrist and immediately halted my steps.

"What, you mad or something?" he asked, as he spun me around to face him. I wanted nothing more than to reach up and slap him and I didn't even know why.

"Why was she here? Didn't you say you ended things with her?" I said as calmly as I could, but I really wanted nothing more than to shout in his face.

"What, you deaf now? Did it sound like I want anything to do with her? So stop trippin' for no reason. Look, I need to talk to you about something," he said, as he held on to both of my hands.

"What a coincidence, because I need to talk to you about something also," I replied as I pouted my lips a bit.

"You wanna go first?" Jaime asked, but I shook my head letting him know he should go first.

"A few days ago, I got a job offer." Just from his tone and the look he got on his face, I knew I wasn't about to like this conversation.

"It's for a new hospital and they need to have a gynecologist to work there, but the contract is only going to be for a year. I think I'd like to go." I knew I wasn't about to like this conversation.

"Well fine, go then," I sassed him, as I pulled my hands from out of his reach in an effort to turn and walk away. Jaime grabbed my hands back and mean mugged me.

"Would you relax, damn. I want you to go with me." I looked at him as if I didn't hear him correctly, but I knew exactly what he just said.

"Go with you, where is this new hospital about to open anyway?" I asked him. This job offer couldn't have come at a worse time. How was I supposed to tell Jaime that I was pregnant when he wanted to take a new job?

"It's in Ghana." I froze as I stared at him for a few seconds without blinking. Jaime waved his hand in front of my face.

"You OK?" he asked me, and I blinked at him a few times, still in shock.

"Ghana, all the way over there?" I began thinking how much I would miss Sammie if I left and went all the way to Ghana. I didn't know about all this, but it was time for me to reveal to Jaime that I was expecting his child.

"Well, as I said, I have something to tell you also."

"OK, let's hear it." Jaime moved away from me and sat down on the edge of my desk.

I exhaled slowly as he waited patiently for me to speak. I reached into my jacket pocket and took out the pregnancy test and handed it to him.

The expression on his face changed to one of shock, or disbelief. I was unsure which one was it. Jaime looked up at me and then back at the test in his hand.

"Th-this yours?" he asked in disbelief.

"No, I normally walk around with random females' pregnancy tests in my jacket pocket. Yes, it's mine silly. I took it just before I came out here." Jaime looked down once more at the test and then a smile spread slowly across his face.

"I'm about to be a daddy?" Jaime was cheesing so hard I couldn't help but smile also.

I nodded my head at him and he rushed to me and hugged me tightly, almost crushing my ribs.

"So you not mad?" I asked, and he pulled away so that he could look me in my eyes.

"Mad, why the hell would I be mad about becoming a father?"

"You don't think it's too soon?" Jaime took my face in his hands and kissed my lips tenderly.

"I don't care if it's too soon or not. You carrying my seed and that's all that matters." I smiled at him and we kissed again.

"Did this happen in Jamaica?" Jaime asked, and I laughed at his question.

"The timing is correct. What are we about to do about your job offer?" I asked him, as he rained kisses on my neck.

"If you don't want me to take it, I won't. I'll stay right here with you guys," he said, as he placed a gentle hand on my stomach.

I thought about what he said and I didn't want to be the reason Jaime didn't take his job offer.

"I'll go with you. I just don't want you to miss out on this opportunity." The both of us kept looking at each other with wide smiles on our faces.

"Let's go take a sonogram so I can see my son." I twisted my face up at him as he took my hand leading us to the examination room.

"Don't start that. How you know it's not a girl?" I asked him as we entered the room.

"Hey, it don't matter to me. As long as our baby is healthy, I'll be a happy man."

I smiled and felt nothing but contented that Jaime was excited I was pregnant. My thoughts wandered off to the fact that we would be moving to Ghana for a year and how much I would miss my sister.

But I knew just as how I had Jaime, she also had King and they would be living together soon since she shared with me her plans of finally divorcing Adam.

Adam Daniel

J sat in the front seat of Officer Alexander's unmarked police car once again.

I had been in total silence for the entire time as we followed King from a safe distance. We had been trailing him now for the last hour or so.

My weapon that I purchased just for this particular job was tucked in my waist.

So far, King had collected his money from two different locations and he was about to collect from a third spot by his crew.

"I say we take him out before he gets home, maybe we could make it look like a drive-by," Officer Alexander said, but I dismissed what he said with a wave of my hand.

We stopped to the opposite side of where King stopped, and I watched as he rolled his window down and one of the guys that stood at the corner walked to his vehicle.

The guy climbed in the back seat after talking with King for a couple minutes. A few seconds after, he could be seen climbing out the back seat and he closed the door.

The money exchange was done just as smooth as the other two. I sat slouched down in the passenger seat, my mind working in overdrive. King's car started up again and we began following him.

"Why you so quiet over there?" Officer Alexander asked, but I didn't bother to answer him. I tried my best to stay focused.

King's car kept driving for over thirty minutes before it came to a stop again, this time in front of what looked like an empty building. There was a car already parked in the parking lot at the building and I watched in curiosity as King and his passenger got out to greet the lady from the other vehicle.

I clenched my jaw repeatedly as my eyes settled on King's ride along guest.

Mrs. Samantha Daniel, sure had a lot of motherfucking nerve. I mean, how long has this been going on behind my back? She out here fucking the enemy all this fucking time.

I pulled my eyebrows together as Samantha spoke to the woman and King stood silently and listened. He began looking around and he spotted the car that I was in.

I watched on as he kept looking at our vehicle. We were parked a far distance from where they were, so as not to draw any suspicion, but close enough so that we could see what they were doing.

I was slouched really low in my seat and the vehicle was tinted enough so that from where he stood, it would be impossible that he saw we were seated inside.

He eventually looked away when Samantha grabbed his hand and they followed the woman inside.

"King got himself a pretty lady there," Officer stupid on my right said. He had no idea that King's pretty lady was my fucking wife.

I closed my eyes and pinched the bridge of my nose, trying my best to hide my anger and frustration.

I tried to jog my memory to see if I missed any of the signs that Samantha was being unfaithful. I tried to remember how many times she said she had errands to run, or she forgot to pick up something at the grocery store.

The many times she said she and Selah had a lunch date and I realized all of those things were probably just bullshit. She had been sneaking away to meet King all this time.

I remembered the day he came to my office and he mentioned Samantha and gave me this smile, a smile that said he knew something I didn't. But I brushed it off, believing he was just trying to fuck with me.

Wait one god damn minute! Samantha was in Jamaica just a month ago, and King was also in Jamaica! So am I to believe that my wife hopped on a plane and went to Jamaica to have some kind of secret rendezvous with this young disrespectful nigga?!

I'd seen enough. "Let's go, drop me off at my office so I can get my car." Officer Alexander turned to me and asked the obvious question.

"Aren't you gonna follow through and get rid of him?" I looked over at him and smiled as he started the car.

"Na, I got an even better idea."

Samantha

I drove home after spending the entire day with King. I was in a happy place. I hadn't felt this alive in a while.

I tagged along with King as he collected his money from his block boys, and let me say this. Selling drugs really was a lucrative business. King collected a hefty sum of money today.

After making his rounds, he and I met with my real estate agent and saw a much better place for my Yoga studio. This one was bigger and had more potential than the first location.

Plus, today was finally the day I would be letting Adam know I wanted a divorce. Our marriage had been basically non-existent for the past few weeks. We'd been seeing each other less and less, barely holding a conversation.

Adam had been preoccupied more than ever and I knew that I had lost him for good now. I believed in my heart this divorce would be for the better for both parties involved.

I, for one, couldn't wait to spend every waking moment with my King. Nothing could keep me away from him; we loved each other and that was all that mattered.

I pulled up to my house and was more than shocked to see Adam's car parked in our driveway. He usually didn't make it home until midnight, and it was not even 8:00pm and he was already at home.

I thought nothing of it. I would just stay out of his way until it was time to go to bed. Then first thing in the morning, I would let him know we needed to get a divorce.

I grabbed my handbag and made my way to the front door and let myself inside. The house was dark as hell as I stepped inside, wondering why Adam didn't turn the lights on.

"Adam!" I shouted out to him as I flipped the light switch on in the living room. I got no reply as I walked through the living room, tossing my handbag on the sofa as I made my way to the kitchen.

I grabbed a bottled water from the refrigerator and stood there as I drank most of it. As I turned around, I almost caught a heart attack at the silhouette figure that stood at the entrance of the kitchen.

"Jesus, Adam, you scared me," I told him, as I placed a hand to my chest. Trying to catch my breath.

Adam stood there and remained still, not saying a thing and barely moving as he looked in my direction.

Creasing my forehead at how oddly he was behaving, I took a couple steps to him. That's when I noticed he was holding something in his hand.

I focused on his right hand and realized he was holding a gun. The two steps forward that I took, quickly turned to three steps back.

"What's going on? Why do you have a gun in your hand?" I asked as I pressed my back into the cold, steel refrigerator door.

"Where were you today, Samantha?" he questioned me, as he began moving closer to where I stood with cat-like steps.

"I-I-I," I began to stammer as I tried to search my brain for a believable lie. But we all knew just how much I sucked at lying.

"Oh, wife, you always were such a terrible liar." Adam was just a few steps away from me now so I eased to my left in an effort to keep as much distance between us as I possibly could.

The gun in his hand was aimed at the floor and not at me, but that could change at any given moment if the wrong thing was said to him.

"I have no reason to lie to you, Adam. I saw a woman earlier today; I have been meaning to tell you, I would like to open up my own Yoga studio," I said, as I continued taking my crab-like steps to the side to stay away from him.

"Yoga studio? How did you plan on paying for this studio, Samantha?" Adam's steps paused, but mine didn't. If I made a mad dash for it, I was sure I could be out of the kitchen and through the front door before he could get to me.

The only problem was that my keys were in my handbag, and my handbag was on the sofa. My cell phone, however, was in my jeans pocket, just in case I needed to call for help.

"Why do you have that gun in your hand, Adam?" I repeated my question to him.

"Tell me something, Samantha. How long have you been fucking Kingsale Rock behind my back?" I froze, my eyes couldn't hide the truth of his statement. How did he even find out about us?

"Ah, they always say your eyes are the windows to your soul," Adam said, as he raised his gun and pointed it at me.

I stopped walking and raised my hands up as they trembled with fear.

"I promise you, I'm not having an affair with King. Please put the gun down, Adam," I said softly, as my voice cracked a couple of times out of fear.

"I knew you were just like her," Adam said, as he got a strange and lost look on his face.

Confused as to whom he meant, I began shaking my head left to right.

"Just like who? Please, Adam put the gun down." I inched to the side closer to the kitchen's entrance.

"My mother was a hoe also, just thinking she could use her body to get men to do things that she required of them. My father was too good of a man for her. Just like I'm too good of a man for you."

I was looking at my husband as if he had lost his entire mind. I knew the story about his mother and I knew for a fact I was nothing like her.

"Adam, you don't love me. You never loved me, you've cheated on me from day one of our marriage. You aren't happy with me. Why do you think it's necessary to continue with this farce of a marriage?" Tears began to roll slowly down my face as I looked at the man that I believed in my heart would have made me such a happy wife and hopefully one day a mother to his kids.

"So you think that makes it ok for you to cheat on me with that Jamaican, cocky motherfucker!" Adam shouted at me as he waved the gun around.

"Would you listen to yourself?! Do you even hear yourself? Adam, you stayed cheating on me during our entire marriage!" I shouted right back at his ass and within the blink of an eye, he was on me.

Adam had his gun tucked under my chin as his cold eyes pierced through mine.

"Out of all the people, you had to cheat on me with the one nigga that I was competing with. The one nigga that was eating my food." Ok, now I was confused. What the hell was he talking about?

"What? What do you mean, eating your food?" I asked, as I searched his face for answers, even as he pressed the barrel of his gun even more into my flesh.

Adam chuckled in my face. "You are the smartest, dumb person I have ever met. You know that Samantha? Do you really think being a councillor would allow me to live this lavish lifestyle I've been living?

"Do you think that this house and all of that expensive shit you enjoy is from me having the one job? I'm in the same line of work as your side nigga." The tears streamed down my face at what Adam was confessing to me.

I shook my head slowly, refusing to process what he just said.

"I don— I don't understand. What are you saying, Adam?" I began to feel nauseous as if I wanted to throw up, the bile rising slowly in my throat.

Adam tapped the side of my head with the barrel of his gun forcefully.

"Think, Samantha, think," he said, pushing my head with his gun again. "I'm saying you've been married to one of the top drug dealers in this community. I run shit, I'm the top dog in this motherfucker. And when I put a bullet through your side nigga's head, I'll be the numero uno... undefeated!" Adam gave a crazy, psychotic smile that had me believing I had been married to a mad man all this time.

"How could do you that? The people in this community, they look up to you, they believed in you Adam. All this time you've been part of the reason the streets have been this way, littered with drugs and people trying to fight off their addiction." I was married to the devil.

"Oh, boo-hoo, Samantha. Who you fooling? And you've been fucking the Jamaican cartel on the side! You ain't nothing but a fucking hypocrite," Adam said, as he dropped his hand with the gun to his side.

Using this small window of opportunity, I lifted my knee and connected it with his balls.

"Aahhhh!" he shouted in pain as he dropped to his knees. Wasting no time, I bolted through the kitchen entrance and ran to where I placed my handbag on the sofa so I could find my keys.

"Fuck!" I shouted, as I realized Adam obviously had moved my bag because it was no longer there.

Hearing his hurried footsteps behind me, I ran for the stairs taking them two at a time. Reaching into my pocket for my cell, I ran into the bedroom slamming the door shut, locking it behind me.

I dialed the one person that I knew would have gotten to me the fastest, my sister.

"What's up sis?" Selah said, as she answered on the first ring.

"Selah, help me, Adam's tryna kill me," I said, as I tried to stay as calm as I could as I heard a loud bang at the door.

"What! What the fuck do you mean he's trying to kill you?! Where the fuck are you, Sammie?" Selah asked, sounding a lot more panicked than I was.

"I'm at home. Please get King and come get me the fuck out of here." As soon as those words came out my mouth the door suddenly came off the hinges as Adam came charging into the room.

I screamed in fright he ran and tackled me like a linebacker; my cell went flying out of my hand onto the floor. Using the barrel of the gun, Adam hit me straight in my mouth.

The taste of blood filled up my mouth instantly. I struggled to fight Adam off, as he straddled me on the ground. I covered my face as he raised his hand to strike me again.

"You wanna act like a fucking slut to that lil' nigga."

Whap!

He slapped the taste out of my mouth, my head flipping to the left. "Then let me treat you like the hoe you tryna be."

The blows that Adam delivered one after the other were too much for me to try and block all of them. My face began feeling numb, my eyes began to swell almost shut.

"Please, Adam, please stop," I cried as I tried in vain to get him off me.

As he pointed the gun at my head, I saw my life flash before my eyes. The kids I'd never have, the happy life I was hoping to enjoy with King.

As the thought of King emerged in my mind, I used the last bit of my strength and I somehow managed to knock the gun away from Adam and it pitched out his hand onto the floor.

As he got off me to retrieve the weapon, I sprung to my feet and raced out of the room. On reaching the stairs, I heard Adam's footsteps behind me.

I turned and looked over my shoulder to see Adam pointing the gun at me. *This nigga has gone absolutely insane*, I thought as I turned back around.

In the haste of trying to make my retreat down the stairs, I missed a step and my body went pitching forward.

It seemed as though I was falling in slow motion; my body felt as though I were somehow flying through mid-air.

I landed with a loud thud and a cracking sound, the back of my head hitting the ground with a bone crushing blow.

I lay there unable to move, my entire body numb with pain.

Just before my eyes began to close, a vision of Adam standing at the top of the stairs looking down at me with his gun pointed at me, was the last thing I saw before I welcomed the darkness.

King

*C*ould life get any better than this?

I sat on my bed as I checked my money, loud ass trap music played in the background as I nodded my head to the beat.

My King pendant swinging on my chest as I thought about Sammie. A smiled formed on my lips and I felt like some love sick puppy. I couldn't wait to live out the rest of my days with her.

I would give all this hustler lifestyle up if it meant I got to fuck with Sammie for the rest of my life. She made me happy as fuck and I wanted to show her just how much I appreciated having her.

My phone began vibrating in my pocket and I knew that it was probably Sammie calling to let me know she was home safe.

I looked at my screen at a number I didn't know. I shook my head and declined the call because I knew a couple of females stayed on that stalker bullshit, calling a nigga from various numbers.

I continued checking my stash and my phone lit up again. I declined that call a total of five times before I finally decided to answer.

"Yoooo, the fuck is this?" I asked, as I answered with a lot of attitude.

"King, I need you to come with me!" a loud, panicked female said on the other end of the line.

I pulled the phone away from my ear and looked at the number again. Nope, I still had no idea who the fuck this was.

"Yo, who this?" I asked, as I dropped a handful of money on the bed.

"It's Selah, Sammie's sister." *The fuck, why the hell was she calling my phone?*

"What's good, ma? Something pop off?" I stood up because something told me I wasn't about to like this phone call.

"It's Sammie. I think something may have happened to her." The hair on the back of my neck immediately stood up. I didn't need to hear anything else before I began putting my clothes on.

"Tell me what happened," I said, as I pushed my feet in my sneakers and grabbed up my car keys.

Almost an hour later, I pulled up to Sammie's home only to be greeted by the sight of an ambulance at the front of her residence.

I didn't waste any time to race out of my vehicle just as I saw a crying Selah at the front door. A body laid out on a stretcher was being wheeled to the back of the ambulance.

"King, oh my god, he almost killed her!" Selah cried, as she followed the paramedics to the ambulance.

I looked down at the body on the stretcher and my stomach did a thousand flips. Sammie looked like she had been run over by a truck. I clenched my jaw as I looked at my girl's face all bruised and busted.

Both of her eyes were swollen shut, her lip was busted open, she had a huge lump on her forehead, and her arm was in a sling. I wanted to run to her but I just couldn't bear seeing her in that condition.

The paramedics wheeled her inside of the ambulance as Selah, with tear stained eyes, was about to hop in along with her.

I placed my hand on Selah's upper arm and stopped her in her tracks.

"Yo, tell me who did this, Selah. So I could go fuck them up." I wasn't even trying to act like the lunatic I felt like at that moment. I said that shit real calm.

"Fucking Adam, that motherfucker did this. I told Sammie so many times to leave his cheating ass alone." I bit menacingly into my lower lip. Adam Daniel was about to be a very dead councilman.

"Aye, don't worry about it. Consider it handled," I said, as Selah climbed inside of the ambulance.

I looked at Sammie. As one of the paramedics placed a breathing mask over her nose, she laid there so still she looked as though she wasn't even alive.

I couldn't even bear to go to her, to talk to her or to even touch her. I allowed Selah to go with her sister to the hospital.

All I was about to do was go hunting for that motherfucker. I needed to find Adam and when I did…he was about to be a dead man!

Samantha

I looked down into the face of a beautiful baby girl. She was so precious with her pretty brown skin and brown eyes.

I smiled lovingly as I held my baby in my arms. The baby I always wanted; she was perfect. She looked up at me and cooed softly and I knew I would give my life to protect her from the ugly world. I would do anything for this precious gift I had finally been given.

Suddenly, the doors to my hospital room opened and two nurses came into the room and took my baby out of my arms.

"Wait, what are you doing? Why are you taking my baby from me?" I cried out as I held my arms out, pleading with them to return my baby.

As they ran out of the room with my baby in their grasp, Adam suddenly walked inside of the room with an evil grin on his face.

My eyes opened as I cried out and I heard someone say my name.

I looked over to see Selah appear from the corner of the room where she was seated.

I looked around, uncertain as to where I was. As I gazed at my surroundings, it became quite evident I was in a hospital room.

I had been dreaming before, but it felt so real.

I looked to my sister who held onto my hand with a worried look on her face.

"Selah, what happened?" I asked, as I tried to move but a shooting pain travelled up my right arm. I looked down only to realize that it was in a sling.

Bits and pieces of what happened to me began to replay in my mind. Adam had gone bat shit crazy and tried to kill me and I fell down the stairs.

"You fell, or Adam pushed you. We aren't certain which it was since you've been in and out consciousness for the last couple of days."

I shook my head, unable to believe that the man I had been married to for over four years would stoop to such unthinkable lengths.

"Selah, it was like he went crazy. He was hitting me, calling me a slut and a hoe. He found about King and I. I don't even know how he did." At the mention of King, I looked around the room hoping that he would be here, but he wasn't.

"Does King know I was hurt?" I asked, wanting to make sure he was alright. I remembered Adam saying he wanted to kill him just as much as he wanted me dead.

"He does, Sammie," Selah said, as she touched my cheek affectionately. The look on her face told me there was more to what she was letting on.

"Well, where is he, Selah?" Taking a few seconds, Selah shrugged her shoulders at me.

"What does that even mean? You don't know where he is?" I felt myself beginning to panic, afraid that something may have happened to King.

"No, I'm sorry, I haven't seen him since the night you were admitted. I don't know where Adam is either. The police are trying to find him." I closed my eyes as my head began to spin and I felt nauseous.

"Are you ok?" Selah asked, as she squeezed my hand. I began cold sweating and I felt the bile rise in my throat, unable to keep it down.

I projectile vomited all over my sister as she screamed out in disgust.

"Shit, thanks a lot Sammie. Let me go get a nurse," she said, as she turned and walked out of my room covered in my gastric juices.

A nurse came a few minutes later with my sister in tow.

"I'm going to get cleaned up and I'll be right back," Selah said, as she walked out of the room. I felt really bad for throwing up on her and the nurse gave me a pitiful look.

"Let's get you cleaned up, Mrs. Daniel." I cringed at the use of my married name.

"Please, just call me Samantha," I corrected her, as she began to tidy me.

"Is my arm broken?" I asked, as I looked down at my injured limb.

"No, it's sprained pretty badly though, but you would be fine." I was relieved I had no broken bones because I knew I had taken a pretty bad fall.

"Your baby is fine also, just in case you were wondering. It's a miracle you didn't suffer a miscarriage." I snapped my head to look over at the nurse.

"What, what did you say? Baby, what baby?" I asked with nothing but shock laced in my voice.

Helping me into a clean hospital gown, the nurse stopped and looked at me.

"Didn't you know you're expecting?" she asked as she looked at me with surprise.

My eyes were unable to even blink as I stared at the nurse with astonishment.

"Expecting? I'm…pregnant?" I whispered the word as though I could hardly believe it myself.

"You are. When you came in we ran some routine blood work and we discovered that you're just barely six weeks pregnant. I guess we assumed that you knew."

I sat speechless as the nurse gave me a worried look. She probably thought I had gone into some type of trance.

"Are you ok?" I made a whimpering sound as the thought finally registered that I was about to become a mother.

King and I were about to parents. This explained the weird cravings for flaming hot Cheetos. I guess our make-up sex in Jamaica was a lot more than just make-up sex!

"I take it those are tears of joy running down your face," the nurse asked, as she smiled at me.

I nodded my head and I smiled back as I wiped the water from my cheeks away. "Well, let me be the first to congratulate you." She touched my cheek lightly before she turned and left the room.

I curled my lips in and looked down at my stomach. It was nothing short of a miracle that I didn't lose my baby from the fall down the stairs.

I really wanted to share my news with King. I didn't even care about Adam anymore and where he could be. I could give a fuck about him. I wanted to be with the father of my child.

Selah walked back into the room with a handful of paper towels and a big wet spot on her T-shirt.

"Oh, Selah, I'm sorry. But do you have my cell?" I desperately needed to try and get in touch with King.

Selah pulled my phone from out of her handbag and handed it to me.

Taking the phone from her reach, I quickly dialed King's number praying he would pick up. The phone rang off the hook until his voicemail came on.

The second time I rang his phone it took me straight to voicemail, letting me he had switched it off.

I didn't bother to try a third time. I handed the phone back to Selah.

"I'm sorry sis, I've been trying to call him since we brought you in. I think he's been trying to find Adam," Selah said.

"I got something to tell you," I told her, as I smiled a little.

"I got something to tell you too," she said, as she smiled right back at me.

King

A nigga was stinking. I hadn't taken a bath in the last two days, but I could give a fuck.

"My youth, promise me when we find this *pussyhole, mek* you take a shower." I looked over my cousin Mark and showed him my middle finger.

A nigga had to call for reinforcement after what happened to Sammie. Mark flew in from Jamaica the next day to help me plan the murder of Councillor Adam Daniel.

That motherfucker was hiding good too. I couldn't find him for shit. The first place I looked was over at Sandy's which I guess would have been way too obvious.

When Mark and I kicked her door down that house was like a ghost town, not a person in sight.

I had all of my niggas searching high and low. I needed to get to him before his crooked ass police friends helped his ass escape.

Then the big break I needed came and I got word on where he would be and who was helping him.

The motherfucker with all the dough and connections, none other than Santa. Word from a very trustworthy source was that Santa had been helping keep Adam and his girl safe by allowing him to stay at his mansion.

He planned on assisting Adam by getting them to leave the country by flying them out on his private jet.

So here was my cousin and I parked out front of Santa's house, it was almost one in the morning and we had yet to see any sign of Adam or Sandy.

I rubbed my bushy beard and ran a hand through my unkempt hair. A nigga hadn't slept in days and I hadn't even visited my girl in the hospital since this fuck boy put her there.

I just couldn't face seeing her like that in the shape she was in. I felt as though this shit was somehow my fault. I felt as though if I had been more persistent that she left Adam, that none of this shit would have ever happened.

That's why it was my duty to fix it, it was my right to make sure Adam never had another opportunity to lay another hand on Sammie again.

"Looks like they about to come out," Mark said, as he pointed at a black Jaguar that was driving away from the house.

Just as I recognized Adam as the driver, my phone began vibrating in my pocket.

I pulled it out quickly and Sammie's name and a picture of her smiling face appeared on my screen. Caught between answering the phone and making sure the car Adam was driving remained in my eye sight, I allowed the phone to ring out.

Tossing the phone at my cousin, I instructed him to switch it off as I followed the Jaguar as it passed my sister's car that I was using.

Mark powered the phone off making sure we had no distractions. Nothing was about to give me greater pleasure than seeing Adam's face when I pumped his body full of lead.

I followed a safe distance behind as Mark smoked a blunt, the weed smoke filling up the inside of the car.

The car headed in the direction of the airport as expected. I touched my waist and felt my burner tucked safely away.

The car stopped at an area away from the regular spot where passengers would be allowed to board their flight. There was a small private jet on the runway awaiting Adam's arrival.

The need for being discreet and unseen wasn't needed anymore, so I was about to drive alongside Adam just as he opened the driver's door and climbed out.

My plan to get rid of Adam and Sandy hit a speed bump when they both reached in the back seat of the car and emerged with a child in each of their arms.

"What the fuck?" I whispered, as I slowed the car to a stop directly to the right of the Jaguar. This nigga had a whole family on the side.

"Youth, you didn't say anything about kids," Mark said, as he turned to look at me.

"That's because I didn't know this motherfucker had kids. Let's go." My car caught Adam's attention and he looked at it curiously just as I opened the door.

Seeing both my cousin and I emerge from the car with our weapons drawn, panic set in on his facial features. He held on to the sleeping child with fear in his eyes as he looked my way.

I walked up to him and Sandy with my gun aimed at the floor, Mark next to me did the same.

"Let me leave with my family, you can go ahead and have my wife. I don't even love her anyway," Adam said, as he cradled the young child in his arms. It appeared that he and Sandy had a set of twins, one girl and one boy.

Adam held the boy and a crying Sandy held the girl in her arms. I wasn't about to involve children in what I had going on with their father.

"I'm about to tell you how this is about to go down. My fam here is about to take your son away from you. Sandy and your kids are about to go in that private jet and fly off to wherever the fuck you planned on going. And you about to come with me."

Sandy began wailing hysterically as Mark walked up to Adam and took the sleeping child out of his arms.

"Aye yo, shut the fuck up with all that crying. You were supposed to be taken out along with him. These kids just saved your life, now get your ass on that plane and don't ever come back," I instructed Sandy. The last thing I wanted was for Sammie to ever find out her disrespectful husband fathered twins. I knew how much she wanted to have a baby of her own.

Finding out something like this would leave her crushed beyond words could imagine. I wanted to spare her that amount of hurt.

"It's ok, Sandy, I'll meet up with you later on." Adam gave his sidechick a head nod and Mark along with Sandy and the sleeping twins walked onto the plane, leaving me alone with Adam.

We eyed each other as I pointed my gun at him, wanting nothing more than to just bust one off and end his life right here on this runway.

"You've been nothing but a pain in my ass from day one. I should have let my dirty cops kill you when I had the opportunity," Adam said, as I walked closer to him.

I smiled at what he said and shook my head. "Could have, would have, should have, motherfucker. Get your hands in the air." He did as I instructed and I felt his waist for a weapon, removing a 9mm.

Without warning, I pulled my hand and cracked him in his face with the butt of my gun.

"Argh, fuck man!" he screamed out in pain as his nose began bleeding.

Just because I wanted to hit him again, I did; this time hitting him with the gun at the side of his head. He fell to his knees as he hollered out in pain.

Remembering Sammie being wheeled into the back of the ambulance, I lifted my foot and delivered a kick to his face, knocking him unconscious.

"*Rudeboy*, you couldn't wait." I turned around at the sound of Mark's voice, as he looked at Adam sprawled out on the cold ground.

"Let's carry this nigga for a trunk ride," I said to Mark. We moved with haste as we bundled Adam in the trunk of Kwana's vehicle.

As we started the car, the plane with Sandy and the twins began making its way down the runway.

"Let's get rid of him, shotta," I said to Mark as we drove off with an unconscious Councillor Adam Daniel in the trunk.

Who was about to be a very dead man!

Roughly two hours later, after Mark and I killed and disposed of Sammie's husband, I made it home, showered and went to the hospital to pay my girl a visit as though I didn't just kill her husband.

When I arrived she was asleep, and I sat in the room quietly watching her as she did so.

I did a lot of dirt in the streets. I'd shot niggas and I'd been shot at. I'd also been to prison but nothing felt scarier to me than the feeling that I might have lost Sammie.

Seeing her on that stretcher proved to me that I really did love this woman and I would stand in front of a loaded weapon to save her.

Sammie stirred in her sleep and I studied her closely as her eyes slowly fluttered open. I remained seated as I continued to watch her in silence. She looked down at her stomach and smiled as she touched it gently.

I knitted my eyebrows together thinking it was something strange for her to do, when she suddenly turned her head in the direction that I was sitting and shrieked out in surprise.

"Shit, King, you scared me. How long have you been here?" she asked, as she put her hand to her chest as I got up and walked over to her.

"A while now, I didn't want to wake you." I examined her face in silence and I felt good to see that the swelling to her eyes was almost completely gone.

Her arm was in the sling and her lip was slightly swollen.

"Why did it take you so long to come look for me?" she asked, with a hurt look on her face.

"I couldn't see you like that. Besides, I was out trying to find that nigga," I told her, talking about her husband.

"Did you find him?" she asked quietly, as she looked away from me. I thought long and hard on how to answer her question.

"Nah, that scary nigga on the run. I didn't find him. I'll keep looking though." I looked her dead in her eyes as I lied through my teeth.

She nodded her head and said nothing. I didn't know if she believed me or not.

Sammie looked at me giving me the biggest smile. "I have to tell you something."

"Oh yeah? Scoot around, let me share this bed with you," I told her, as she shifted her body to the side I laid down in bed with her, bringing her closer to me. She laid her head on my chest as she continued to speak.

"My sister's pregnant." I looked down at the top of Sammie's head in a bit of surprise. Because I knew her sister broke up with Lamar.

"For that nigga Lamar?" I asked as I stroked her back, my body finally being able to relax after the last couple of days I had.

"Na, her boss." I scrunched my face up because I was confused as fuck, but I decided to leave it alone.

"Guess who else is going to become a mommy?" I closed my eyes as I felt myself drifting off to sleep.

"Who?" I asked not even giving it any thought about who she could be talking about.

"Me."

My eyes flew open and I pulled Sammie away from my chest so that I could look directly in her face.

"Yo, what you just say?" I asked. My face said it all as Sammie smiled broadly at me and nodded her head.

"You're about to become a daddy." She beamed at me and I felt like my heart was about to burst out of my chest.

"Was that why you were rubbing your stomach earlier?" I asked, as I looked down at her belly and placed my hand on it.

"You saw that huh?" She lifted her head and kissed my lips. I was fucking ecstatic hearing I was about to have a child of my own.

"I promise you, you just made me the happiest nigga alive." I reached in and hugged her tightly, kissing her neck.

"You my Empress, you know that right?" I asked her as I caressed the face of the woman I had fallen madly in love with.

"And you're my Jamaican King."

EPILOGUE

Samantha (One Year Later)

I locked up the doors of my Yoga studio and made my way out to the parking lot.

King stood cradling a screaming Marley in his hands. I giggled at the expression King had on his face as he tried in vain to get his son to settle down.

"Aw, come here little man. What did daddy do to my baby?" I cooed, as I took my screaming son from out of his father's arms.

"Man, fuck what I said about you going back to work. You need to stay at home and take care of that bad ass little boy until he starts to walk," King fussed, as he opened the door to his Mercedes as I hopped in the back with our son.

I shook my head as I undid the buttons of my shirt so that I could breastfeed Marley. I smiled happily down at my son as he latched on to my nipple.

Marley looked just like Kaden did when he was this age.

King and I moved to Jamaica about a month after I found out I was pregnant. King left his life of being a drug dealer behind and opened up his very own restaurant when we moved to Jamaica.

Kwana and Kaden also moved back to Jamaica and lived not far from where we lived.

Selah was a proud mother of a baby boy and was currently engaged to Jaime. She and Jaime would be coming to visit us soon as his contract at the hospital in Ghana came to an end.

I was finally able to open my Yoga studio and these Jamaican girls loved taking my classes so they could do all their crazy Jamaican dance moves a lot easier.

Adam was never to be found after he assaulted me. I knew someone could not just disappear into thin air, and my gut instinct told me King had something to do with it. I never pressed him for any information though. I decided to leave well enough alone.

I looked down at the ring on my finger and blushed. Sometimes it felt surreal that King and I were now married.

I looked at my husband as he drove us home and thought to myself that I never would have believed that the first time we met that he would be the husband and the father of my kids.

Because we planned on having as many kids as we could.

Sometimes life throws a curve ball at you. I thought when I married Adam he would have been my happily ever after.

Turned out I was wrong. The love of my life was a bit younger, and a lot more hood than I expected.

This was the story of how I met my Jamaican King!

THE END......

NOTE FROM THE AUTHOR

I just want to thank you guys for reading about Kingsale and Samantha's journey to find love. Sometimes love comes in a form we may not expect, as in the case with Samantha falling for someone a bit younger than her.

I hope you enjoyed reading this book as much as I enjoyed writing it. Please leave me a review when you're done reading.

Below is a sneak peek to my next release!

SNEAK PEEK: DESTINY AND TRENT/ A HOOD WEDDING

Prologue- Trent

Yeah…Yeah…Yeah…Yeah

I'm just a bachelor, looking for a partner,

Someone who knows how to ride, without even falling off.

I gyrated my hips slowly to Ginuwine's song "Pony" for a room filled with screaming women at the house where I performed for a bachelorette party.

"Yasss, Dingo, come over here honey." I turned my head in the direction of the voice that belonged to a woman so skinny, I feared she may have some sort of eating disorder.

But I wasn't here to judge anyone and their eating habits. I was here to make as much money as I could and leave to get back home to my family.

I plastered a smile on my face that probably said I cared about this chick as I rotated my hips, as I made my way to where she sat on a chair in the living room. When I fact I could give a fuck about her or any of the other thirsty females in this room. What I did want was the fistful of money she was waving at me.

With my eyes focused on her, I bit down on my lower lip as I stood before her. I could see the obvious lust on her face and in her eyes as she eyed my well-endowed package, barely contained in the briefs I wore along with a pair of cowboy pants.

"You wanna touch it?" I asked, as I boldly took her hand in mine and slowly glided it down my tight, well-sculpted stomach in the direction of my rock hard dick.

Her eyes grew huge as fuck as I purposely made my dick jump as her fingers ran across my rigid organ.

"You like that?" I asked her, as she nodded her head vigorously as she tucked her money inside of my brief underwear.

"Squeeze him, he likes that shit." I licked my full lips as she looked up at me and squeezed my bulging dick. I blew her a kiss and she all but fainted as I walked away to find my next victim.

So how exactly did I end up stripping again when I was supposed to have left this life behind me? I mean, I was in a wonderful relationship with Destiny and I was now the father of bouncing baby boy.

So what the fuck was a nigga doing in this private party gyrating my hips and thrusting my dick in these bitches' faces?

Well, it all started when a nigga asked Destiny to be his wife.

I swear after that…shit went downhill from there!

Coming Soon………………

ABOUT THE AUTHOR

 Hi…my name is Candy Moore. I am 38 years old and I am a single mother of two girls. I reside in the Caribbean country of Trinidad and Tobago and have been signed to Royalty for about a year now. I love being a Royalty author! My hopes and dreams is to become an author full time, and to be able to one day hit that number one spot and have a huge following of reader's. My first official release under Royalty was Just another Two faced Chick. One thing I can safely say about my writing, is that I switch it up…. You won't get the same storyline with every book I drop. I love giving my reader's something different! feel free to like my page on Facebook: Authoress Candy Moore to be the first to know what I'm working on.

Royalty Publishing House is now accepting manuscripts from aspiring or experienced urban romance authors!

WHAT MAY PLACE YOU ABOVE THE REST:

Heroes who are the ultimate book bae: strong-willed, maybe a little rough around the edges but willing to risk it all for the woman he loves.

Heroines who are the ultimate match: the girl next door type, not perfect - has her faults but is still a decent person. One who is willing to risk it all for the man she loves.

The rest is up to you! Just be creative, think out of the box, keep it sexy and intriguing!

If you'd like to join the Royal family, send us the first 15K words (60 pages) of your completed manuscript to submissions@royaltypublishing-house.com

LIKE OUR PAGE!

Be sure to <u>LIKE</u> our Royalty Publishing House page on Facebook!

CPSIA information can be obtained
at www.ICGtesting.com
Printed in the USA
LVHW022141150319
610814LV00004B/407/P